"THIS IS THE WAY IT SHOULD BE WHEN A MAN MAKES LOVE TO A WOMAN . . ."

There was only an instant for Tracey to recognize the dangerous timbre in his voice before he'd pulled her close, molding her against himself as he bent to kiss her. The kiss was an expert sensual onslaught, and his strong hands moving roughly, sensuously, over her aroused feelings in her body that she'd only guessed at before. And suddenly there was no time to think as passion surfaced in both of them and the world became an enchanted place . . .

SIGNET Books by Glenna Finley

AFFAIRS
OF
LOVE

by

Glenna Finley

Friendship is constant in all other
things save—affairs of love.

—SHAKESPEARE

A SIGNET BOOK
NEW AMERICAN LIBRARY

TIMES MIRROR

NAL BOOKS ARE AVAILABLE AT QUANTITY DISCOUNTS WHEN USED TO PROMOTE PRODUCTS OR SERVICES. FOR INFORMATION PLEASE WRITE TO PREMIUM MARKETING DIVISION, THE NEW AMERICAN LIBRARY, INC., 1633 BROADWAY, NEW YORK, NEW YORK 10019.

SIGNET TRADEMARK REG. U.S. PAT. OFF. AND FOREIGN COUNTRIES REGISTERED TRADEMARK—MARCA REGISTRADA HECHO EN CHICAGO, U.S.A.

SIGNET, SIGNET CLASSICS, MENTOR, PLUME, MERIDIAN AND NAL BOOKS are published by The New American Library, Inc., 1633 Broadway, New York, New York 10019

First Printing, September, 1980

1 2 3 4 5 6 7 8 9

PRINTED IN THE UNITED STATES OF AMERICA

1

Anyone less determined then Tracey Winslow would have been thoroughly intimidated when she walked through the doors of that London hotel on a rainy morning in early June.

The gray stone building had been a fixture of Piccadilly since 1906 and its imposing outlines still reeked of Edwardian opulence. The lobby was just as impressive, with marble columns, gilded Louis XVI furniture, and a staff which must have been apprenticed to Lord Nelson even before Trafalgar.

Most American tourists who strayed into the place by mistake lost no time in getting out again—often stumbling over the worn but priceless carpet on their way.

It's true that Tracey hesitated, but merely for a look at the museumlike surroundings before she walked across to a long counter near the doorway. It was made of marble and could have doubled for a soda fountain in a Midwestern town. This one, however, was presided over by the hotel's hall porter and his uniformed minions.

She picked the gray-haired man wearing the most gold braid and told him, "I'd like to see Mr. Jennings, please. Bartholomew Jennings. He's a guest here."

"Might I say who is inquiring?"

"Miss Winslow," she replied, lifting her nicely molded but determined chin to show she wasn't intimidated by his offputting tone.

He pursed his lips then and made a production of turning to a wooden rack behind him, finally extracting several messages from one pigeonhole. "I believe you called earlier, Miss Winslow. We notified Mr. Jennings when he came in. That was some time ago." The timbre of his voice and his expression conveyed that Bartholomew Jennings had plenty of time to get in touch with her if he'd wanted to.

Tracey deliberately ignored the implication. "I'm glad to hear that he's in the hotel. It will be easier if I call him on a house phone. If you could show me where they are . . ." She looked around as she spoke.

"Mr. Jennings isn't in his room just now," she was informed austerely. "If you'd like to leave another message, we'll see that he receives it, Miss Winslow."

"I'd really rather not," Tracey confessed. "I don't want to bother the man—all I want is to ask him for an interview. I promise that it won't take more than three or four minutes of his time." She saw the look of indecision on the hall porter's face and pressed on. "I'd be terribly grateful."

The porter reluctantly recapitulated to the stark entreaty in her gray-green glance. "Well, there's a chance you could meet him. Unannounced, mind you. I hate to disappoint a nice young lady."

His comment wasn't surprising. Men of all ages had been succumbing to her appeal on a fairly consistent basis since Tracey had graduated from college three years before. In the interim, a certain amount of cynicism might have tempered her outlook, but time hadn't dimmed anything else. Her complexion was lovely enough to warrant a second glance even in London, where women excelled in such things. Tracey had also inherited delicate features and lips that curved into a heartwarming smile—like the one the porter was basking in just then. And if his avuncular beam was any indication, he was even approving the fiery color of her hair. Tracey would have preferred to have been born with a subdued auburn shade rather than a gleaming copper, but she tried to overcome its effect by wearing it in a neat casual style for daytime, and letting it flow loose only for evening occasions.

Just then, she was wishing that she'd spent extra time in achieving a sleeker version that morning and that she'd worn an outfit which made her look more soignée than a tweed suit topped by a practical nylon raincoat.

But although she had no intention of admitting it, Tracey hadn't much hope of bearding Bartholomew Jennings in his den—let alone the august surroundings of his London hotel. As a best-selling American writer, he had no need for personal publicity and made a point of eschewing it. For generations, members of the Jennings family had done their best to stay out of the limelight. Rumor had it that they weren't enchanted when Bartholomew, after earning a history degree, achieved considerable success with his first historical novel. His second effort had been even more lucrative, and after that he turned out popular and well-written books almost annually. The sparse publicity issued by his publishers revealed only that their elusive writer was in his early

thirties and unmarried. The pictures on his book
jackets showed a thin-faced, dark-haired man wearing black-rimmed glasses and an austere expression.
Tracey knew that he wasn't in the habit of granting
press interviews regarding his writing, but since he
was also an acknowledged expert and collector of
Early American furniture, she'd wanted to garner
his views on the London antique market for an article. Her stack of traveler's checks had grown alarm-
ingly thin after a month's travel on the Continent
and she needed another article to impress her editor
and restore her finances.

Her desperation must have shown, because the
hall porter became positively hearty as he leaned
over his marble counter and said in a low voice, "I
just happened to notice Mr. Jennings having coffee
in the lounge when I passed a few minutes ago." He
jerked his head toward the wide corridor to his right
with a worn but still impressive Oriental carpet running down the middle.

"You mean . . . a public lounge?" Tracey asked,
scarcely able to believe her luck.

He nodded. "Just opposite the main lifts. It's very
well known in London." His expression regained a
fraction of earlier haughtiness. "Surely you've heard
of our afternoon tea served there?"

"Oh, yes. Of course." Tracey crossed her fingers
behind the full skirt of her cinnamon raincoat. She
certainly wasn't going to confess that she hadn't
adopted the British custom of afternoon tea during
her brief stay. If it helped to get an audience with
the elusive Mr. Jennings, she'd drink it on the hour
and even remember to pour milk into the cup first
in true English fashion. "Thanks so much for your

help. I'll go down there." She brought her crossed fingers up into view. "I hope it works. . . ."

He winked. "The best of British luck, miss."

Tracey grinned and marched purposefully down the corridor he'd indicated. There were tempting display windows on either side of it filled with goods from the neighboring Mayfair shops, but she didn't hesitate, knowing that her quarry might escape if she wasted time.

Her steps slowed abruptly as the corridor widened and she saw the lounge that the hall porter had mentioned. It loomed impressively to her left, a high-ceilinged room which looked as if it should have been listed as one of the British Museum's treasures. There were pink marble columns and a chandelier which might have graced the palace at Windsor. Fragile-looking gilt chairs upholstered in pink *peau de soie* were carefully arranged at damask-covered tables. Behind them was a fountain where water trickled around a marble female figure of Rubenesque proportions. The only outward sign that the lounge was a commercial establishment was the uniformed waiter depositing a silver coffeepot on a table in front of an elderly couple. Tracey's gaze moved swiftly over them and stopped when it reached a masculine figure at a table in the back corner. The man was frowning as he concentrated on a catalog propped against the edge of the table. While she watched, he reached out for the pot of morning coffee in front of him to refill his cup. The fact that there was nothing in it sank in belatedly—only after he'd replaced the pot and raised his cup for a swallow. His black scowl made Tracey choke with laughter.

That *did* penetrate his consciousness, and he

raised his head, transferring the scowl to her even as the waiter moved hastily over with a full pot.

Tracey realized tardily that she had started off wrong with her quarry. And it *was* Bartholomew Jennings—there was no denying that thin face and the shock of dark hair which became even more rumpled as he raked it back from his forehead. His gray-eyed glance narrowed behind his glasses and he obviously debated against getting to his feet when she paused by his table.

"Mr. Jennings?" Every evidence of the laughter was gone from her voice by then; it was all she could do to keep her tone from quivering with nervousness.

A sigh of resignation came from the man in front of her as he got to his feet. "I'm Jennings. Do I know you?"

"Not really. My name is Tracey Winslow." Her glance encompassed the telephone-message memos he was using to mark the pages in his catalog. "I've been trying to get in touch with you for the last couple of days."

"Winslow?" He saw the direction of her glance and his expression cleared. "I thought your name was familiar," he admitted dryly. "I'm not giving interviews on this trip. That's why I didn't return your calls. Now, if you don't mind, I'd like to drink my coffee before it's completely cold—like the toast." He took time to frown down at two thin pieces of dry bread in a silver toast rack.

"Oh, please, I know this is an imposition . . ." Her voice trailed off. Clearly, feminine appeals didn't cut any ice as far as the man was concerned. And it didn't look as if he planned to invite her for coffee. He stood resolute, waiting for her to leave.

Tracey didn't cooperate. She stayed where she was, letting her gaze go swiftly over him. He was wearing a dark green tweed jacket that looked comfortable but hardly Bond Street. The rest of his garb was equally casual—flannel slacks, a gray shirt, and a subdued wool tie. Her glance moved back to his face and she saw that his expression hadn't changed; it still wasn't sociable. She took a deep breath and tried another line of attack. "I know you don't like to talk about your writing, but Mr. Jorgensen said you might not mind discussing antiques with me."

"Oscar Jorgensen? The publisher? What's your connection with him?"

"I'm a writer. Trade articles," she said hastily. "Not in your line of country at all. I'm sort of a stringer for his publications. When I talked to him about some articles from the Continent and Britain, he mentioned you were in London."

Bart Jennings gave her a hooded look. "Oscar suggested you contact me?"

Tracey opted for the truth. "Not really. As a matter of fact, he didn't think you'd want to bother. But my budget's lean, so I thought I'd try."

Jennings surveyed her almost grimly and finally glanced at his watch before saying, "How about fifteen minutes? I'm expecting company after that."

"You mean it?"

"Sit down before I change my mind." As he pulled out a chair for her, the waiter materialized at her elbow with another cup.

"More toast, sir?" the man asked, going around to pour coffee for both of them.

Jennings looked across at her questioningly.

"No, thank you," she said. "Coffee will do just fine."

He nodded and shoved his glasses more firmly on his nose as he turned to the waiter. "No toast." He gestured toward the rack. "And you can take that away."

"Very well, sir."

They watched him remove the rack with its unappetizing contents before gazing across the table at each other with transatlantic understanding. "Now, then"—Jennings resumed his brusque tones—"what do I discuss for fifteen minutes that will fatten your purse?"

"How about recent developments on the British antique market?" Tracey suggested, reaching hurriedly for a pad and pencil.

"Depends on what you're looking for. There's probably more cranberry glass in New Jersey these days—same thing goes for brass chamber sticks. The prices are astronomical, but that isn't anything new. There's no use generalizing," he added, fixing her with a "don't-bother-me-anymore" expression as he reached for the catalog he'd been reading earlier.

"Oh, please"—she leaned forward before he could open it—"you can't back out now. I was stuck writing trade articles for a carpet magazine for months until Oscar finally let me try something else. If I have to go back to extolling the glories of nylon shag, I swear I'll—"

"Jump off the bridge into the Thames?"

"Unless there's a toll on the bridge."

"Things are that bad?" Something flickered in his glance, and he put the catalog back on the table. "Okay—then we'd better dredge up a topic for you. Although why you teenagers choose to visit Europe on a shoestring is beyond me."

"Teenager!" She started to laugh. "Good Lord, I'm twenty-three."

"Then you're old enough to know better."

"Now, look—I'm not so strapped for money that I'm loitering on street corners. I would just prefer not to phone home for emergency funds."

"Then there *is* somebody at home to help you out? Parents? Family?"

"My parents are dead, but Oscar would certainly cable some money."

"I didn't realize you knew him so well." The words were out before he was aware of how they sounded, but he couldn't miss the wave of red which swept over Tracey's cheeks or the ominous jut of her chin as she said stiffly, "Not that it's any of your concern, but Oscar is an old friend of my family's. I can see now why he discouraged my contacting you."

"I'm sorry if I got the wrong impression. . . ."

"You certainly did. Very few women behave like the heroines in your novels, Mr. Jennings. I know that you sell more books when females leap into a different bed in every chapter, but most of us don't live that way." Tracey's attack wasn't entirely legitimate, because the Jennings heroines were remarkably chaste and discriminating when compared with the competition. His darkening expression, however, showed that she'd touched a vulnerable spot. Recklessly she plowed on, "If that's the way your mind runs, the hotel should keep you chained to the chair."

"They don't worry unless it's a full moon or I've eaten too many bananas. You can simmer down, Miss . . ." He sneaked another look at the memos. "Miss Winslow. I didn't bring my gorilla suit with me this trip." He went on in a level tone, "I've heard that redheads were combustible. You certainly live up to the reputation."

His words made Tracey recall suddenly that she was in no position to act as "critic at large" to the man across the table. Not unless she wanted to be thrown out on her ear. "I'm sorry, Mr. Jennings. Honestly, I don't make a habit of being rude to people."

"I have the feeling that it was mostly my fault. Probably because I don't like cold toast for breakfast."

"So you decided on a half-baked reporter instead?"

His eyes narrowed behind the glasses but there was no missing the glint of amusement in them. "Your words—not mine. There's not much you can get out of all this for your notes, is there?" He reached across idly to pick up her notebook and studied it. "Ever done any research on graphology?"

His abrupt change of subject startled her almost as much as his action. "Handwriting? No—not really. Those notes are just to jog my memory—they won't mean much to you."

"I don't know about that." He studied the writing with care. "There's a definite leaning toward malnutrition."

"I beg your pardon!"

"It shows in the way you slant your letters and the overly disciplined capitals. Of course, it could be a tendency to indulge in sexual fantasies. Don't say that you haven't been warned." He seemed amused by her openmouthed reaction as he slid the book back across the table. "No charge for the service. It's a hobby of mine."

"Sexual fantasies?" she muttered inanely.

"No. Handwriting." He had some trouble keeping

a solemn expression as he switched his attention to the pamphlet she'd left on the table when she was extracting a pencil from her purse. "Are you going to attend this sale later?"

She had trouble keeping up with him. "The antique flea market in Piccadilly? I don't know—I just picked up that brochure from the hall porter's desk. It doesn't sound like a bad idea."

"Generally there isn't much of value on display," he warned, "but sometimes there's a happy surprise."

He bent forward to hand the pamphlet back to her, and as Tracey retrieved it, her sleeve caught the top of her cup. "Oh, no," she moaned as coffee slopped onto the tablecloth and splashed down to her lap. She stood up and brushed at it futilely with the back of her hand. Then Bart was beside her, using an immaculate damask napkin to vigorously brush down the front of her skirt.

"Really, it isn't necessary," she insisted, embarrassed, and stepped back out of reach. "The tweed is practically indestructible and I was tired of the color anyway."

He looked up then, frowning, but when he saw her flushed face he merely gestured toward her chair and gave the coffee-stained napkin to the hovering waiter. Bart waited for the table to be reset with a clean cloth and their cups refilled before he sat down again himself.

"I'm terribly sorry," Tracey started to apologize, but he cut in before she could go on.

"Forget it, Miss Winslow." He gave her a considering glance as he added, "There's a chance I can be free for dinner in a day or so if you're serious about an article. I'll have to change my plans somewhat before I can say definitely."

He broke off as a clear feminine voice came across the lounge, "Bart, darling, I thought you were going to be waiting."

Her vowels were perfectly accented but the tones would have reached Green Park if the beautiful blond marching up to their table had breathed more deeply.

Tracey hurriedly stuffed her pencil and pad back in her purse as the newcomer stared down at her, assessing the soggy skirt with unerring accuracy. Since the blond was wearing a tailored green tartan suit together with a pale yellow cashmere turtleneck, there wasn't even a token competition. Especially since she also possessed a gorgeous complexion and flaxen hair pulled back in a simple but elegant chignon.

Bart Jennings had gotten to his feet and Tracey realized that he'd made a conventional introduction which involved "Miss Frome" in the middle of it. Even as she started to say hello, the blond gave her a cursory nod and said, "Bart, I *did* promise that we'd be there for lunch and the doorman wasn't happy about my blocking traffic when I parked." She favored Tracey with a cool smile then. "I'm sure Miss . . ."

"Winslow." Tracey's smile was equally cool.

"I'm sure Miss Winslow will excuse us."

Bart didn't look enchanted with the situation, but there wasn't much he could do about it. Almost grimly he summoned the waiter for the check. Tracey took the opportunity to fade away, but Bart stopped her before she'd retreated more than a step or two. "Just a minute, Miss Winslow. About that schedule we were discussing—I'll be in touch."

Tracey started to beam as his words registered.

"You mean it?" she began, and then remembered the blond who was frowning at this new development. "Thank you," she substituted deftly and favored both of them with a dazzling smile. "I'll look forward to it."

"Don't forget your pamphlet—for the antique flea market," Bart reminded her, handing it to her.

"I'd memorized the address, but I'd better have it just in case."

"You're on your way there now?" Jennings asked.

Tracey nodded, but before she could reply, the other woman put a possessive hand on Bart's forearm. "Speaking of being on the way, darling . . ."

"It was nice to have met you, Miss Frome. Goodbye, Mr. Jennings," Tracey said, and walked away. The head porter was in the corridor when she reached the revolving entrance door.

"Did it work, miss?" he asked almost anxiously.

Tracey's lovely smile flashed. "Yes, thanks. At least near enough." She didn't want to linger too long in case Bart and his blond were on her heels. "Thanks very much for your help."

"My pleasure. If you want a taxi, miss, you'd do better to have the doorman help you at the other entrance."

"I'll walk, I think." Tracey tightened the belt on her raincoat as she peered through the glass door panels. "I don't have far to go."

There weren't many pedestrians when she reached the sidewalk of the famed London street. Not surprising, she decided, since it was a cloudy Sunday morning. Most of the people who'd braved the overcast weather were tourists strolling along looking into attractive display windows. A few Piccadilly merchants were open, mainly booksellers with pic ture postcards or small knitwear shops tempting visitors with their cashmere displays. The wrought-iron gates of St. James's Church were also open but Tracey settled for admiring the garden alongside, since a glance at her watch showed that the church service was almost over.

Tracey tried to keep her thoughts on church history as she read a polished plaque telling about Londoners' fortitude during the World War II bombings, but her gaze was preoccupied. Her abstracted air must have been more evident than she realized, because an elderly church warden came over and asked solicitously if he could help her in any way.

Tracey recovered and blushed furiously. "No, no, thank you," she said, trying to sound matter-of-fact. "I'm just fine." She did manage to drop some coins in the poor box under his approving glance before she walked back to the sidewalk.

It was still too early for the antique show but not too early for lunch, she told herself—especially since she needed to pass some time. There was a flourishing fast-food shop on Haymarket and a few minutes later Tracey was happily consuming a hamburger and coffee, surrounded by young Europeans who conversed in three or four languages while they ordered burgers and shakes as if they'd invented them. Tracey smiled ruefully when she'd finished the last bite of her own lunch and rose to leave. Fine thing! She traveled all the way to London for food that she could have eaten around the corner at home. On the other hand, her day's budget was still relatively unscathed, which meant she could shop with more than enthusiasm at the antique flea market. Especially now that there was the possibility of a story from Bart Jennings. He certainly hadn't looked enchanted at the thought, but he *had* promised. From the determined set of Bart's chin, she doubted if even that gorgeous blond could convince him to alter his chosen course.

Tracey started to chuckle at the idea and then came rudely back to the present when two German couples carrying laden trays lingered purposefully by her booth.

"I'm just going. You can have this place," Tracey assured them, catching up her purse and leaving them in possession. No doubt they would be discussing what strange people the Americans were after she'd disappeared. Especially a woman who was sitting alone and giggling. Thank heaven, she hadn't been talking to herself!

The gray leaden skies had lightened by the time she reached the street again, and while it was a far cry from early summer weather, Tracey unbuttoned her raincoat and enjoyed the gentle breeze as she walked back toward the famous statue of Eros in Piccadilly Circus. The antique market was being held in a Regent Street hotel just beyond the busy intersection, and Tracey crossed the streets carefully, forcing herself to look right instead of left. London authorities had even painted warnings on the pavement as an extra precaution for transatlantic visitors.

When she reached the hotel, she found the antiques fair well-advertised, with sidewalk signs directing visitors up to a mezzanine, where vendors had set up stalls in big conference rooms and an adjoining high-ceilinged ballroom.

Tracey paid the nominal admission fee and, in return, was given a mimeographed sheet with rough locations of the stalls and sellers. She glanced over it quickly, not surprised to find several dealers from Scotland and Wales. The small-town merchants had evidently decided there was a better market in London at the beginning of the tourist season than at home. Certainly the buyers looked anxious to spend money, and most of the accents were American.

While Tracey was deciding which way to go first, she was amused to hear a bohemian type say to his companion, "There's no point wasting my time looking at Tiffany lamps—I'm just not a stained-glass person." Tracey decided that he apparently specialized in stained vests instead, as the one he was wearing still bore remnants of lunch.

She hid a grin as she walked through the first room to linger by displays of porcelain and antique jewelry. At first glance, most of the buyers seemed to be in her own price range—rock-bottom cheap. The dealers looked resigned to this turn of events and sat chatting among themselves, more interested in their cups of tea than attempting the hard sell.

Tracey ignored the tables of expensive silver, trying instead to find Victorian ivory oddments that harbored Stanhope lenses—a favorite of hers. If held up to the light, the little peepholes revealed surprisingly clear views of the Wheel at Blackpool, the Sailors' Home at Liverpool, or an occasional Niagara Falls.

Dealers had been cool to such bric-a-brac until they discovered that American collectors were intrigued by the miniatures, and then prices had risen sharply. Tracey didn't have any luck with her inquiries until she reached the displays in the ballroom and encountered a dealer with a crude ivory cross showing a purported view of the Garden of Gethsemane.

"It's not in tip-top shape," he admitted. "But if you want it, you can have it for five pounds."

Tracey knew that it was overpriced, but her good sense warred with a desire to add to her collection. If she ate another hamburger for dinner rather than the roast beef she'd promised herself, her finances would come out about even. "I'll take it," she said, digging down for her wallet. "Do you know of any other dealers who might have some Stanhopes?"

"You'll have to ask around," he replied, losing interest as soon as the five pounds changed hands. "It's novelty stuff and most of them don't bother with it. Now, if you wanted something really worthwhile, I could put you onto a good thing."

Tracey looked up from storing the cross in a zipped section of her purse. "What did you have in mind?" she asked dryly.

Her sarcasm was lost on the man behind the table. He bent toward her, leaning one hand on a worn velvet case of Victorian fish knives as he confided, "Furniture, that's what. A Regency piece from one of the stately homes on the south coast. Mind the flex . . ." he cautioned as she moved out of the way of an overweight man carrying two cups of coffee down the aisle behind her.

"The flex?" Tracey frowned, trying to figure out what the dealer meant. Her expression cleared as he impatiently gestured toward an electric extension cord at her feet. "Oh, that." She stepped carefully aside. "Thanks. Now—about this furniture—is it on display here?"

"Among this muck? Not likely. You know Kensington High Street?" As she nodded, he lowered his voice to a confidential tone. "There'll be a piece at the Antiques Arcade there tomorrow."

Tracey shook her head, visualizing a massive dining-room table or sideboard. "I can't cope with getting furniture home. The freight costs put it right out of my class."

"I'm talking about a small piece," he insisted. "Mind you, they're a real investment these days. This is a Regency worktable—just right for storing those Stanhopes you collect, or sewing bits and pieces."

"Regency worktables come high—awfully high these days. Thanks for telling me, but I really can't afford—"

He cut in brusquely, "The one I'm talking about is only . . ." and named a price that was ridiculously cheap.

Tracey almost told him that she wasn't straight off the boat and he needn't try to sell her Tower Bridge for an encore. Before she could say anything, he pulled a small photograph from his coat pocket and shoved it in her hand.

She saw a charming Regency worktable with a rectangular top and two D-shaped leaves that would delight any collector or interior decorator. Tracey chewed her lower lip thoughtfully and then she asked, "This will be in the High Street tomorrow?"

Her awed tone told the man all he wanted to know. He took the photograph from her fingers and replaced it carefully in his pocket. "That's right, miss. 'Course you'll have to get there early. A bargain like that beauty won't last long. London's no different from any town in that."

Tracey nodded absently as her thoughts raced. There might be a better story here than anything Bart Jennings could provide. The worktable either had to be stolen merchandise, if genuine, or someone was turning out creditable fakes to lure the tourists. Either way, it was an angle to tempt her publisher. "What time does this shop open?"

"It's not a proper shop. We've a temporary display in the arcade until we get things arranged." He tore a strip from a pile of newspaper and penciled a figure on it. "Here's the stall number. Down the stairs at the arcade and toward the back. Ask for Nigel. He'll be there at eleven. One thing, though," he added. "He'll want cash. Simplifies the bookkeeping—if you know what I mean."

"I'm beginning to." Tracey folded the piece of newpaper and put it in her purse, wishing she could wash her hands afterward. By then, she was thoroughly annoyed with his innuendos. It was hard to sound eager and cooperative as she said, "All right, I'll be there around eleven."

The man gave a satisfied nod. "One more thing. I'll have to tell him your name—so he'll know you're serious about the merchandise."

"Winslow," Tracey said, after debating whether to substitute "Smith."

"I'll pass the word along," he said, and moved away to the other end of his display table, where an elderly man was examining a demitasse service that had seen better days.

Tracey walked on through the crowded aisles, but her collecting urge for Victorian items had disappeared when she considered what was in store for her the next day. Belatedly she realized that she should have asked the stall owner's name so that she'd have something tangible to back up her research. She turned and walked back to where she'd bought the cross, but found the display table deserted.

A bearded man behind the adjoining stall leaned over to ask, "Can I help you, miss?"

"Not really," Tracey told him. "I wanted to ask the other man something. The one who was here just a few minutes ago."

"He had to leave—asked me to watch his stuff."

"Then you don't know when he'll be back?"

"Haven't a clue," he assured her cheerfully, and turned his back as a woman in front of his table indicated she wanted to see some jet beads in a small display box.

"Damn!" Tracey said under her breath. Then she moved determinedly toward the front entrance of the antiques fair as another possibility occurred to her.

She waited until the line of people paying admissions had disappeared before approaching the woman who sold tickets. "I wanted to get in touch with one of your dealers, but he's gone to lunch and no one knows exactly when he'll be back. Do you have his name and the address of his shop? He's at the second stall inside the ballroom door to the right."

The woman's expression underwent a sudden change. "I'm sorry, we're not allowed to give out that information. If you'll leave your name and telephone number, I'll try to see that he gets it. *If* I have a chance."

"But he knows my name. . . ."

The woman shrugged. "Then that's all that can be done. How many, madam?" she asked, craning her head to speak to a woman who had just arrived.

Tracey stepped aside after bestowing an annoyed look on the ticket-seller, who ignored it. By then, she and the newcomer were deep in conversation about

the terrible spring weather. Tracey had heard the
same discussion ever since she'd arrived in London
and knew the dialogue by heart. She also knew that
getting the ticket-seller to volunteer any more information was about as likely as arranging a special
showing of the Crown Jewels.

When she reached her hotel by Hyde Park Gate
some time later, she was happy to find her room was
comfortably warm, thanks to the portable electric
heater plugged in by her bed. Tracey hung up her
raincoat and ran a glance down the television listing
she'd left atop the small set by the window. Apparently she'd have plenty of time for dinner, since
the BBC promised only a discussion of Common
Market ailments and a spirited educational session
on how to prune roses.

For a moment her thoughts drifted to Bart Jennings and his blond Miss Frome. Probably they'd be
planning where to have dinner about now. She'd say
that it was hard to beat Mayfair for decent food, but
there was a fascinating new *trattoria* in Knightsbridge if he wanted something different. Of course,
there was always Soho . . .

Tracey was so engrossed in her story line that the
sudden ringing of the telephone scarcely registered.
She stared at it, bewildered, until it pealed again
and then dived for the receiver before the unknown
caller could hang up. Even a wrong number would
be a welcome change. "Hullo?" she said breathlessly.

There was a pause. Then a deep masculine voice
said, "Miss Winslow?"

"This is Miss Winslow." Tracey hesitated as well,
before taking a wild guess. "Mr. Jennings?"

"That's right." He became brisk and businesslike.
"This is my second try—evidently the hall porter

copied down the wrong number for you on one of those memos."

"I'm sorry . . ."

"There's no reason to be."

Tracey grimaced. She should have known that Bart Jennings would not suffer fools gladly. The hotel porter had made the mistake; why should Tracey apologize?

". . . hadn't meant to leave in quite such a rush," he was going on, and Tracey concentrated to catch up. "Unfortunately Stella chose to abandon her car in the middle of the street rather than bothering to park it." He paused, letting Tracey know by his tone what he thought about that.

"I imagine the doorman was upset," she said, trying to say something diplomatic.

"So was the policeman who'd just walked up."

"Not a very good way to start the day," Tracey commented, feeling unaccountably cheered but determined not to let it show in her voice. "It's a good thing you weren't driving."

"I hope I'd have better sense," he cut in, setting her straight on that score. "But that wasn't what I called you for. I'm sorry that I'm tied up for dinner tonight but I can manage lunch tomorrow if you'd like to get on with the story ideas. If you could meet me at eleven-thirty—say, here at the hotel—we could beat the crowds. I'll make a reservation right away."

On the point of accepting happily, Tracey suddenly remembered the Kensington High Street arcade and her appointment. "I'm sorry, Mr. Jennings," she said slowly. "I can't. I've made other plans. Just a little while ago."

Tracey could almost feel the waves of surprise coming through the phone wire, and when he finally replied, there was a dry undertone to his words. "Can't they be changed? The other plans, I mean. I won't be in town long and I thought this was important to you."

"It is. Terribly important. I wasn't fooling about that. But this other thing sounds like a terrific story." Her voice rose tremulously. "You see, there was a dealer at the flea market today who told me about a Regency worktable at a ridiculously low price. I'm supposed to see it at the Kensington High Street arcade tomorrow at eleven by asking for somebody named Nigel. Even if I took a taxi afterward, I couldn't make it to your hotel by eleven-thirty."

"How much is the worktable?"

His question was so abrupt that she blinked and automatically parroted the figure she'd been quoted.

There was an impatient mutter before Bart announced, "That's completely unrealistic. Obviously the thing's either a fake or stolen."

"I *know* that." Indignation made her voice crisper than she realized. "But don't you see the story possibilities?"

There was another distinct pause. It could have been that he was thinking over those possibilities, or it could have been that he was shaking his head and counting to ten. When he spoke again, it sounded as if the latter option was correct. "All I can see is that you're sticking your neck out a hell of a way unless you have solid facts to back up your accusations later."

"Naturally I wouldn't—"

"And I wouldn't try any trumped-up articles on Oscar," he went on as if she hadn't even spoken. "Libel laws can break you. He won't thank you for getting his publication involved."

"I have every intention of—"

"Think it over," he said, cutting in again. "I'd hate to see your career blasted at the very beginning. If you change your mind about lunch, you can phone me here in the morning."

"Don't plan on it." Her frosty rejoinder was interrupted when his receiver was slammed down. "Damnation!" Tracey fumed, and scowled as she replaced her own phone. From the way Bart barked out orders, he must have been doing it since kindergarten. She tossed her head and went over to pick up her purse on the bureau before she went down to dinner. If he thought she was going to give up a promising story just for the chance to eat a decent lunch for a change, he was more of an egotist than she thought. She could only hope that Stella Frome got a filet mignon or roast beef out of her duties! The woman deserved it.

It was a good sales talk and it carried Tracey through the appetizer for her meager dinner in the deserted dining room of the hotel. The main course of mince, a British euphemism for hamburger, was accompanied by an omelet which was frizzled on the outside and still runny on the inside. Halfway through, Tracey laid down her fork in surrender. At that moment, she would have abandoned a Pulitzer prize for one dinner that hadn't been scorched, undercooked, or left to congeal before serving.

She was still hungry when she watched the fascinating ramifications of rose pruning and aphid assaults an hour later, so she demolished a candy bar she'd stashed for an emergency. One more count against Bart Jennings, she decided grimly when getting ready for bed. Or to be more accurate—one more inch around her waistline, thanks to a candy-bar diet after his warnings on malnutrition. And it had to be malnutrition, she told herself, because she certainly wasn't suffering any sexual fantasies—no matter what her handwriting said.

She sighed as she got under the blanket. For a day that had started pretty well, it had finished in the dregs.

2

Tracey awakened the next morning to note a pale band of sunlight rimming the shade at the hotel window and felt unaccountably cheered even before she got out of bed.

Closer investigation showed that the sun was indeed trying to get established. It was having a time slipping between the clouds, but there was a break of blue now and then which promised hope for a real touch of summer.

When Tracey descended to the dining room for breakfast dressed in a green corduroy suit and a white cashmere turtleneck, the young Italian waiter beamed and ceremoniously seated her in a bay window where she could look out on the park.

In such pleasant surroundings, she managed to ignore the watery poached egg, concentrating instead on piping-hot tea and scones with raspberry jam. She toyed with the idea of calling Bart and saying that she'd changed her mind about lunch—that she could make it, after all. Then she saw a determined Englishman in a bowler striding along the sidewalk, and the firm set of his jaw made her think again. If she gave in, Bart would probably say "I told you so"

26

when she called and read her a polite lecture as soon as she arrived at the hotel.

Her reasoning wasn't logical, but it did serve to get her on a bus a little later headed for Kensington High Street instead of Piccadilly. She was early but there'd be no chance of changing her mind or getting cold feet once she was on the scene.

When the red rover jerked to a stop and let her off close to the arcade, she saw that there was still an hour before the eleven-o'clock appointment.

The High Street was already thronged with shoppers and the busy restaurants and food stores showed the influence of the Mid-Eastern visitors in yashmaks and turbans who lived in the area. Pita bread was stacked in display windows of eating places and the aroma of freshly brewed coffee came through open doors of small shops.

The Londoners managed to politely overlook the Mid-Easterners as they did the millions of visitors from other parts of the world who thronged the city each summer. Women in tweed suits and sensible shoes marched into the big department store nearby, obviously heading for a "cuppa" rather than sampling the smaller restaurants along the busy street.

Tracey went into a bank and cashed a sizable handful of traveler's checks so she'd be ready in case she actually had to buy the worktable. The maneuver would scuttle her spending money, but if the story were worthwhile, no doubt Oscar would come to the rescue.

With the pound notes safely tucked into her wallet, she went back out on the street again. She tossed a mental coin between wasting time in a coffee bar until eleven or looking into the attractive antique shops in nearby Church Street. Church Street won,

and she turned the corner at the parish church of St.
Mary Abbots with its unusual vaulted cloister, to
wander up the winding country-style street. Shade
trees at the curbs and blocks of attractive small
houses which looked as if they'd been moved straight
from a village setting seemed strangely at variance
with the noise from the buses along the busy thoroughfare.

Tracey forgot about the modern-day sounds as she
peered into the nicely arranged display windows of
the antique shops on the block. Most of them specialized in furniture or mirrors, it seemed. Victoriana
was the popular period, and the discreet price tags
showed there weren't any giveaways. The pound
notes in her wallet wouldn't even have made an acceptable down payment on most items, and Tracey
felt a twinge of dismay—she was on a wild-goose
chase and probably the only thing she was going to
get out of it was another budget lunch.

Her spirits improved when she lingered by the
window of a shop specializing in china and small ob-
jets d'art. A tiny ivory cribbage board with carved
feet was especially appealing, and she went in to inspect it more closely. The shop's proprietor was as
intrigued by the piece as she was, saying that it had
just come in and wouldn't last long. Tracey nodded,
ruing the day when she'd heard about Regency
worktables. A quick look at her watch made her say
a hasty good-bye, knowing that she'd have to hurry
to get back to the High Street arcade by eleven.

The clock on the corner struck the hour when she
was just a block away, and Tracey dashed into the
big antiques mart a minute or so later.

She pulled up and tried to appear fascinated by a

display case of old crystal and jet beads while she got her breathing under control.

"See anything you like, love?" asked an overweight woman behind the counter. "I've more stuff back here. Just puttin' it out."

"You mean jewelry?"

"What else?" The other gestured around her. Every available inch of the stall was covered with antique jewelry. By then, she was staring at Tracey warily. "What did you have in mind, dearie?" she asked, shoving her cash box prudently out of reach.

"Furniture. And I'm looking for a man named Nigel."

The woman shrugged. "Never 'eard of 'im. You'll 'ave to search around."

Tracey started to ask another question, but by then the woman had bent over a stuffed shopping bag, clearly finished with her part of the discussion.

The other stall holders who were in evidence on the first floor weren't able to help either. One or two looked up from their newspapers long enough to say that they were just helping out for the morning and didn't know anybody's name. The stall number she mentioned didn't even make sense, they claimed.

Tracey was tempted to give up. Then she discovered some shadowy stairs at the back of the arcade where a sign said "MORE DISPLAYS THIS WAY."

Rent must have been cheaper in the basement, because the landlord clearly wasn't wasting electric light bulbs or heat on the premises. There were bigger sections, however, and Tracey felt a new surge of hope as she saw furniture stacked all over the floor.

The first stall holder had to be pried away from a cup of tea, which he was drinking behind a display of brass beds. He rubbed his chin when she asked whether he knew anybody named Nigel. He hesitated so long that Tracey was about to move on in disgust when finally he said, "Happen I do. In the corner." He jerked his thumb as he spoke, and then picked up his tea and retreated behind his beds once again. She stared after him, a "thank you" dying on her lips. For a mad moment she wondered what he'd do if she said she was interested in brass beds, as well. Then she chuckled as she took another look at the huge Victorian pieces. If she moved one into her apartment, she'd have to walk over the mattress every time she crossed the bedroom.

She was still smiling when she reached the display of furniture in the far corner the man had indicated. Her hopes zoomed upward as she noticed a nice burl walnut side cabinet with a marble top almost hidden behind an alabaster statue of a dancer that had suffered a chipped elbow and was missing a knee.

Tracey had just decided that the statue really deserved a decent burial instead of a new owner when a man emerged from the rear of the stall. He was in his early thirties, with dark hair and mustache, wearing well-fitting tweeds. "Are you interested in that period?" he inquired with a suggestion of an Irish accent.

"The dancer, you mean?" When he nodded, she shook her head, confessing, "Not really. I'm not even sure what period it is. At home, we'd call it 'late Depression' or 'early Coolidge.'"

He smiled in agreement. "I know what you mean. Over here we call it Victorian, for a place to put the blame. Her Majesty will probably come back to haunt us someday." He leaned against the side cabinet as he went on. "If it's not alabaster you're wanting—what strikes your fancy?"

"Actually, a worktable. Regency. I was told Nigel would know of one." She looked at him hopefully. "Have I come to the right place?"

"That's right. I'd almost given you up."

She smiled. "Next time, leave a paper trail. Finding you was like threading the Hampton maze. Is the table here?"

"Just behind the curtain." He led her to the back of the display, where dingy burlap screened a small area. There was a single-element hot plate on a metal counter behind it. Tracey noted the inevitable teakettle and pint of milk beside it before her attention was drawn to a delicate worktable by the wall. She drew in her breath sharply as she went closer to admire it. It was even nicer than she could have imagined—from the short brass-tipped flared feet to the lovely patina on the D-shaped mahogany leaves. Even a reproduction would be priced far higher than the figure she'd been promised. For an authentic Regency, the amount was ridiculous When she checked the price a moment later, though, Nigel confirmed the quote.

"Mind you, we're selling at a tremendous loss, but my boss is liquidating his inventory. He won't sell to the trade—says he wants to see the good pieces go to some deserving people . . ."

He broke off as a young woman pushed aside the curtain. She looked surprised to see Tracey, murmuring, "Sorry, Nigel. I didn't know you were busy. There's a message for you. You're to call this number. They say it's important."

The bland expression disappeared from Nigel's face like a wave washing over a sandy mark on the shore. "Right. Thanks, love." He took the paper from her hand, saying, "Maybe you'll show Miss . . ."

He looked impatiently at Tracey, and she replied automatically, "Winslow."

"Of course. It just slipped my mind. Show Miss Winslow to a chair out front. I'll be back in a tick."

Tracey followed obediently, sitting on a chair by the front aisle of the display. The woman gave her a perfunctory smile before walking away.

Tracey would have liked to slip back and inspect the worktable more closely, but knew very well that Nigel intended to prevent just that by moving her out. She nervously checked in her purse to make sure that her wad of pound notes was still safe, and managed to drop her address book in the process. It was when she bent to retrieve it that she saw a piece of paper half-hidden on the floor under the oak commode nearby. The paper turned out to be a freight invoice for a Napoleon III side cabinet destined for an address in the United States. The shipper was listed as Nigel Pelham, Ardsley House, in . . . Tracey frowned as she tried to make out the smudged name of the town. At least the "Hampshire" which followed was clearly written. That couldn't be too hard to find.

Carefully she shoved the invoice back to its original position on the floor. She had barely straightened in her chair when Nigel came down the stairs and hurried toward her. He smiled when he saw she was watching him, but even as Tracey got to her feet, she could feel the difference in his manner.

"I'm sorry to have kept you hanging about all this time, Miss Winslow. Especially now that I have to disappoint you. That was the old man on the phone—it seems the worktable's been sold."

"Oh, no!" She had no trouble sounding annoyed, but it didn't have any visible effect on the man beside her. He stayed where he was, as if screwed to the floor. Apparently there wasn't even going to be a substitute offered.

Nigel's next words confirmed it. "And there's nothing else that you'd care about, I'm sorry to say. Actually, the worktable was the last of a lot. The heir to one of our stately homes needed a bit of quick cash—death duties and all that."

"I don't suppose you know of any other dealers who might have something good to offer . . ." Her voice trailed off as he shook his head and turned to go. She reached out to catch his coat sleeve. "Would you mind if I took a last quick look at that table? So I could remember the features if I find another one?"

She started to move past him, only to find her own sleeve caught in a firm grasp. "Sorry, Miss Winslow. I got a rocket from the old man to have it packed and out of here. Unless I want to be unemployed, I'll have to get on with it." He turned her toward the stairs and walked with her. "You might find something in Church Street. At least, give it a go."

Since he stayed at the bottom watching her, there wasn't anything Tracey could do except nod with apparent good grace and trudge up the stairs to the first floor.

She walked out to the street again and let herself be carried along with the other pedestrians while she faced the fact that her attempt at investigative reporting had turned out to be a dismal failure. She had no story, no worktable, and worst of all—no lunch. The last disaster came to mind when she heard the chiming of church bells and checked her watch.

"Damn, damn, damn!" she swore softly, but a

woman walking past gave her a wary look. Quite clearly, well-bred Londoners didn't go down the sidewalk talking to themselves!

Tracey's shoulders straightened as she thought about it. So she wasn't a well-bred Londoner. She was an uncouth American tourist—and a starving one besides. A sudden recklessness made her decide to treat herself to an elegant lunch in Knightsbridge. It was cheaper than a visit to a psychiatrist, and that's what she'd need if she dwelt on her inadequacies much longer!

She felt immeasurably cheered by her rash decision and decided to blow the budget and take a taxi rather than queue for a bus. "Chicken today, feathers tomorrow," she thought recklessly, and walked over to the curb, looking for a vacant cab.

There were people all around her—some in line for the bus stop to her left, others just waiting for a break in the traffic to cross the wide street. Cars and buses were almost bumper to bumper as they went by—so fast that Tracey nearly missed an empty taxi cruising the middle of the street.

She saw it at the last minute and waved frantically, to get the driver's attention.

At the same time he acknowledged her signal, she heard her name called behind her. Confused, she turned to search the crowd with her glance, convinced she was imagining things.

When she saw Bart Jennings elbowing his way through the swollen bus queue, trying to reach her side, she could hardly believe her eyes. She heard him shout, "Stay right there," and she turned back to wave away the taxi pulling in to the curb. Just then, she felt a distinct shove in the middle of her back.

Tracey teetered wildly on the curb, trying to regain her balance, and then gasped as she staggered into the street. A woman in the crowd screamed, but the noise disappeared under the squeal of brakes from an approaching double-decker bus.

The red radiator loomed up, and in another second Tracey knew she was going to be draped over it. As her eyes closed to shut out the horror, she felt herself yanked back onto the sidewalk so hard that she almost sprawled flat the other way. Her eyes flew open again and she discovered that her nose was pressed against a man's belt buckle. She tried to get back on her feet, smudging an immaculate white shirt with her lipstick in the process. By that time she was almost beyond coherence. "Oh, God!" she moaned. "What a mess!"

"Take it easy, honey. You're okay. Try to stop shaking." It was a brusque male voice in her ear and it evidently came from the owner of the white shirt, who was leaving bruises on her upper arm as he stacked her upright again. "No matter what you've heard about me," Bart Jennings was going on in a soothing tone, "there's no need to throw yourself at my feet. I'll be happy to settle for considerably less."

3

Tracey knew he was trying to give her time to collect herself so that she wouldn't weep all over his shirtfront, as well. She tried to reply in the same vein but could only manage to gulp nervously and shake her head.

"Poor little thing." This time, it was a wizened old lady with a shopping bag who was looking anxiously at Tracey. "There's a chair in the store behind you, love—if you'd like to sit down."

"I'm all right, thanks." Tracey managed to smile at the woman before looking up appealingly at Bart. "Could we get out of here—everybody's staring. I feel like a fool."

"Okay. There's no problem." He flagged a cab in the middle of the street, which had been caught in a sudden standstill of traffic. "Come on, let's get that taxi," he said crisply, and put an arm around Tracey's shoulder as he hustled her out to it. He took care to allow plenty of leeway for the bus, which was still stopped by the curb.

"Park Lane," Bart directed the taxi driver once they were inside the cab and he'd closed the door. "Just beyond Hyde Park Corner." The driver nodded and shoved the meter down as they started off. Bart turned to survey Tracey, who had sagged on the leather seat. "Sure you're okay? You didn't actually get bumped, did you?"

"No. Thanks to you." She tried to smooth her hair. "I think I turned gray when I saw that bus bearing down."

"You'll have to remember to look to the right when you step off the curb. I know it's instinct to do the opposite, but—"

"Wait a minute," Tracey cut in, unwilling to be blamed for what had happened. "I didn't step off that curb, somebody shoved me—hard. I almost went flat on my face."

"Good God! No wonder you look like a ghost. So much for polite bus queues."

"That wasn't what I meant . . ." Tracey broke off in confusion. "Anyhow, there was no real harm done—thanks to you," she repeated lamely.

Jennings brushed that aside, almost impatiently. "You mean you saw who did it? Why didn't you say so? We could have reported it." Then he grimaced, realizing how futile the gesture would be.

"Forget it. I'm not even making sense." Tracey took her lipstick from her purse, only to decide that her fingers were still shaking too much to apply it.

"You'll feel better after some food."

"Probably you're right." She put the lipstick back and replaced the purse by her side. "You can drop me off anywhere along here and I'll get a cab back to my hotel. I don't want to be a nuisance."

His eyes became thoughtful slits. "If I didn't know better, I'd think you *did* get a whack on the head. You're having lunch with me. That's the purpose of this whole affair."

Tracey's already racing pulse spurted hopefully at his words, but she probed a little further—to make doubly sure. "But you must have had other plans. Just because you bumped into me doesn't mean that you're obligated to feed me."

"Obligated, hell! What do you suppose I was doing on the High Street in the first place?" He went on brusquely. "I was trying to catch up with you before you wasted an entire month's salary on some fake antique that you'd pay duty on when you got it home because the varnish was still wet."

Since Tracey was feeling like something scrubbed and hung out to dry, she forgot about polite behavior. "I must have made a dandy first impression on you," she flared at him. "Two minutes after we'd met, you were accusing me of being Oscar's favorite doxy. Now you're insinuating that I don't know an antique from an aardvark. Well, thanks very much, but I can take care of myself."

A telling silence followed her declaration until she remembered the lipstick smudges still decorating his shirt. She grimaced then and gestured toward them. "I'm sorry—I guess I lost my temper. Honestly, I don't usually behave so badly!"

His stony expression softened. "In pro football they'd rule that you had been drawn offside—so you can scrub the apology." As the cab slowed in front of a Park Lane hotel, he sat forward and reached for his wallet. "Here's where we're lunching. What do you say we eliminate hemlock from the menu and try a martini instead?"

Tracey waited until they were both on the sidewalk and he'd paid off the cab before saying, "My clothes don't match this neighborhood."

"You look fine." He buttoned his sport coat over

the offending smudges on his shirt and nodded toward the hotel entrance, where two Arab guests in native garb were getting in a limousine. "Besides, around here the clothes scene is changing."

"Just like the High Street. If I didn't know I was in London . . ."

"Exactly." Bart gave her a sideways grin. "At least, you can still drink the water and most of the natives understand us."

Tracey thought about that when they'd been installed in the nicely decorated grill room of the hotel, where the red of the leather chairs was repeated in the waiters' uniforms. She waited until two iced martinis were delivered and then smiled at Bart across the starched tablecloth. "You're wrong about the natives understanding us. I haven't heard an English accent since we walked in the door."

"Probably because Italians like to work in London. That should make the lasagna a good bet," he said, surveying the menu. "Unless you're still feeling shaky and would rather have something bland and easy to digest. Maybe an omelet—" He looked up, surprised, as she started to laugh.

"I'm sorry," she got out, using her napkin to wipe her eyes. "But if you knew how many omelets I've eaten since I've been in this town, you wouldn't even mention the word. They're nourishing and cheap," she explained, seeing his puzzled look. "Hamburgers are a mistake here unless you hit the fast-food chains."

Bart's answering grin made him look five years younger. "Say no more. When I traveled the first time, I never got out of Chinese restaurants for the same reason. They're usually safe and cheap all over the world." He broke off as the waiter came to take their order, and didn't even consult Tracey before saying firmly, "Roast beef, baked potatoes, and a green salad."

She nodded thankfully and sat back while he settled the rest of the menu. Bart fitted more into the role of a successful businessman than he had the day before. His sport coat, a muted gray check, was worn with nicely tailored flannel slacks. The collar of his shirt fitted as if it had been custom-made on Savile Row, and the plain gray silk knit tie looked just right. In fact, she decided, there was no touch whatsoever of the slightly absentminded writer she'd met in the coffee lounge the day before.

"Is your martini all right?"

She blinked and noticed that he was staring back at her across the table with some amusement. Apparently he'd noticed her preoccupation and had left her to it.

"Oh . . . yes, thanks." She took a hasty swallow to prove it and almost choked in the process. "I was trying to think why you looked different," she said after she'd pulled herself together. "It's because you're not wearing your glasses."

"You won't have to cut my meat for me, if that's worrying you. Generally I just wear them when I have a lot of reading to do." He took pity on her flushed face and changed the subject. "What in the devil are you doing over here on your own? I should think somebody would be keeping closer track of you."

"You've written so many historicals that you're living in the wrong century," she told him flippantly. "Ever since we've had the vote, women have been allowed to wander."

"I'll remember, but you didn't answer my question."

Her gaze wavered at his gentle reproof. "There's a great-aunt I'm supposed to visit if I get to Edinburgh. She's about eighty now. Very fond of violets," she added absently.

"A lot of elderly ladies in Britain like to wear flowers."

"Well, I've never seen her *wear* any violets," Tracey said carefully, to set the record straight. "She eats them. Candied ones. It made a great impression on me when I was ten."

He took a swallow of his drink as if he needed it. "I was about to suggest that the hotel doctor check you over as a precaution."

"I know. I could tell by your expression. You looked as if I'd suddenly sprouted another head." She grinned unrepentantly and sipped her martini. "Do we have to go on being discreet, or can I tell you what happened at the arcade?"

"Since I'm buying lunch, I intend to call a few of the shots. Roast beef first, and the sordid details over dessert. Unless something vital's due to happen in the next half hour or so."

She shook her head. "Absolutely nothing. I struck out all the way around."

"Cheer up. You've just joined the rest of the world," he replied calmly. "Here comes the waiter with our soup. Let's concentrate on food."

It was idiotic that such prosaic words could make so much sense or that afterward Tracey could feel so much better. When she took the last bite of her *crème brûlée*, she said, "That's the most delicious meal I've had since I set foot in this country. I feel like a new person. Almost strong enough to face the

lemon-liver casserole they're serving at my hotel
tonight."

"Just take it one meal at a time." Bart waited then
until a waiter refilled their coffeecups and they
were alone again. "Okay—since you've been momentarily restored—what happened in that damned arcade?"

She frowned as she tried to remember. "The Regency worktable was there, and it was beautiful. The
price Nigel what's-his-name quoted was just what I'd
been told. But when I was about to reach for my
wallet, he was given a telephone message." Tracey
bit her lip as she thought about it. "He said it was
his boss. Anyhow, when he came back, the sale was
off. Apparently the worktable had already been
sold."

"Did he try to foist anything else off on you?"

"Just a quick trip to the front door," she admitted
ruefully. "He couldn't get rid of me fast enough."

"And you think the worktable was genuine?"

"I'm practically sure of it." She met his glance
squarely across the table. "Which meant that it had
to be stolen. That man knew what he was doing. He
said something about reducing the inventory, but
that was just flimflam."

Bart Jennings rubbed his thumb along his jaw-
bone. "You've made me curious. Would you mind
going back to the arcade with me once we've finished
here? Do you have time?"

Tracey nodded. She almost said that she didn't
have anything else on her schedule for the next week
unless he counted sightseeing tours or visits to the
Tate and the British Museum. "I can manage it and
I *would* like your opinion on the rest of his stock.

There wasn't anything I could see that compared with the worktable."

"Right." Bart flagged a waiter and asked for their check. "Maybe it will be an exercise in futility, but at least we can corner your Nigel again and see what he has to say. I gather he wasn't the same person you'd met yesterday at that flea market in Piccadilly."

"No. Nigel was the first team. The other man was a different . . ." She broke off, her expression suddenly serious.

Bart looked up from signing their lunch check. "You were saying?" He frowned as he noticed her pale cheeks. "What's the matter?"

"Nothing. At least, I don't think . . ." she began, and then added quickly, "I know it's crazy, but mentioning that man from Piccadilly—I'm almost sure he was in that bus queue behind me."

Bart didn't reply immediately. He finished with the lunch check and waved the appreciative waiter away before he said quietly, "I think you've had a shock. There may have been somebody who looked like the same person."

She bunched her napkin and put it on the table with restrained force. "You don't have to be so diplomatic. Why don't you just come right out and say that I'm imagining things?"

"Because I'm not sure that you are. Let's take a look at the scene of the crime first. Want any more coffee? . . . No? Then, let's go."

He kept the conversation on strictly neutral territory during the cab ride back to Kensington High Street, ensuring that they didn't get into anything more controversial than who had the best chance at Wimbledon later in the month. Tracey discovered that for a man who made his living writing about the past, Bart possessed a strictly twentieth-century mind. Her preconception of a fusty scholar who'd put out the milk and bring in the cat was completely wrong.

He was also treating her more carefully than during that first meeting. Either he was acting the perfect gentleman after her near-miss with the bus, or, manlike, he didn't want to trigger her temper again. Tracey pressed back into her corner of the taxi seat and wished that she had curbed her impulsive words on the way to lunch.

Bart frowned as he noted her quiet manner. If she'd only known, he'd been more amused than aroused by her early flare-up. Her obvious apprehension as the cab slowed to let them off at the Kensington arcade was making him wonder about the wisdom of the return visit.

But Tracey led him unhesitatingly toward the entrance after he'd paid off the cab, as if determined to see it through. "There's no reason for us to spend much time here," he told her almost brusquely once they'd gone inside. "If I remember, most of the stuff is priced as high as the traffic will bear."

"You're probably right. Come on, let's go down to the basement. The woman over in that jewelry stall is already convinced that I'm a suspicious character. She probably thinks we've come back to case the place before the heist."

"I don't know why. The Salvation Army wouldn't give most of this stuff house room." He jerked his thumb toward a display of warped tile-top tables. "Those wouldn't have won a design prize when they were new. Unfortunately, that stuff is going to the States by the container-load these days."

"Maybe it's to get even for some of the stuff we've shipped over here," Tracey said mildly as she led the way down the stairs. "I wonder if Nigel is still around—they seem to be pretty casual about staffing in this place."

"That's not the only thing they're casual about. Why in hell don't they turn on some lights? You should have told me to bring a flashlight."

"It's easier to sell some antiques in the dark." She nodded to their left. "Especially a brass bed."

Bart saw a price tag and whistled softly. "The Prince of Wales couldn't have afforded that one. Do people actually buy these things?"

Tracey rubbed her finger along a walnut bookcase. "Well, they don't dust them—that's for sure. Nigel's stuff is in this next display." She moved ahead and peered past a poster bed. "Darn, there isn't anybody around. Wouldn't you think they'd be afraid we'd steal something?"

"It would take a derrick to get most of this stuff up the stairs." Bart's gaze was cynical as he surveyed the haphazard display. "Where was that Regency worktable of yours?"

"Behind that burlap curtain. Do you think it's all right to poke around, Mr. Jennings?"

He stopped to give her an incredulous look over his shoulder. "What did you say?"

"I just wondered if we should—"

"Not that," he cut in impatiently. "The 'Mr. Jennings' bit."

"Oh." Warmth flooded her cheeks again. Tracey could feel it and wished that she didn't blush like a simpering ingenue every time the man looked at her. "What should I call you? 'Bartholomew'?"

"Not unless you want to walk home," he said grimly. " 'Bart' will do fine."

He started toward the curtain once again, and this time Tracey trailed on his heels. After all, she told herself, if anyone objected, they could always claim to be searching for Nigel.

"Looks as if he's closed up shop," Bart said, stepping back to avoid the dust that rose when he pulled back the curtain to look around it.

Tracey nodded. The hot plate was still in place, along with the teakettle, but someone had appropriated the milk and there was an empty space where the worktable had been standing.

Bart let the curtain fall back as they retraced their footsteps to the front of the stall. "I'm afraid we'll have to count it as a lost cause. Why don't you wait here while I scout around and see if anybody knows where to reach this Nigel of yours. There's a chair over there."

"That's where I waited before—when I saw the address," Tracey said. Her expression brightened. "I'd forgotten about that paper. I wonder if it's still there. No—damn! Somebody must have seen it."

"What in the deuce are you talking about?" Bart had followed her and stood frowning as she straightened after checking the oak commode. "You can't like that thing! Whoever owned it must be still celebrating."

"It *is* awful, isn't it?" Tracey said, following his glance. "But I meant the invoice I saw under it. I'd forgotten about it until now. You don't have to ask about Nigel," she continued smugly. "I've already found out his source of supply. At least they picked up a Napoleon III side cabinet from someplace called Ardsley House in Hampshire. I'm not sure exactly where, but it shouldn't be too hard to find. What's the matter?" she asked, looking up at Bart's puzzled face.

"You're sure it said Ardsley House?"

"Of course. I had plenty of time to read the invoice before I put it back." She stared at him with dawning comprehension. "Do you know the place?"

"I've never been there," he said slowly, "but I've met the owner, Oliver Rustad."

"And he does have a Napoleon III side cabinet?" Tracey probed with growing animation.

"I imagine so. His estate is supposed to be one of the showplaces of the south coast. But that isn't what's important. . . ."

Her gray-green eyes were shining with excitement. "You mean there's more?"

"I'm not sure," Bart said carefully. "I *do* know that I was talking to him at two o'clock this morning. I even told him about your appointment here to meet Nigel and view a Regency worktable."

Her lips shaped a soundless whistle. Then she said, "Of course, it *could* be a coincidence."

Bart made a noise that could only charitably be called a snort and took her by the elbow, leading her to the stairs. "Don't be a damned fool! When you open up a can of worms, lady, it's time to go fishing. You might even end up with a bigger catch than you planned."

4

There wasn't any more conversation until they reached the High Street again. Tracey paused automatically at the curb, thinking that Bart would call a taxi to take her back to her hotel or, hopefully, mention another meeting before he left her on the sidewalk.

Instead he took her elbow and said, "Let's go across and have a cup of coffee in that department store."

"But we just *had* a cup of coffee."

"I need time to think, and this isn't the place," he said, indicating the crowded sidewalk. "Besides, they sell other things besides coffee."

After such an enigmatic reply, Tracey didn't dare question him further. She did manage to study his thoughtful profile as they waited for the traffic light. He appeared totally unaware of the stream of traffic which coursed both sides of the busy thoroughfare, ranging from taxis and buses to a pushcart labeled "My Streetcar Named Desire." The thronging pedestrians were just as varied in type, going from twin sets and conventional tweed coats worn by British matrons to saris and cardigans on their East

Indian counterparts. Nearly all the shoppers were laden with plastic shopping bags, and the younger ones were pushing strollers or hanging on to toddlers as well. Even so, several managed to give Bart's tall, lean figure an appreciative glance as he tugged Tracey into the department store he'd mentioned.

She went along obediently and waited until they were served in a coffee bar on one of the upper floors before she said, "This is really going from the sublime to the ridiculous."

"You know, I think you're right," he said, taking one sip of the bitter brew and pushing it away. "Okay, I'll level with you. I'm not keen about the 'coincidences' today. Especially this Ardsley House development. Five will get you ten that the phone call to your Nigel came after Oliver had talked to me."

Tracey's glance widened as the import of his words registered. "But the accident on the sidewalk. Surely you don't suspect he had anything to do with that?"

"Damned if I know." Bart took another swallow of coffee and then seemed surprised that he'd been so foolish. He pushed the cup away again as he leaned toward her across the small table. "Oliver was telling me about the brutal taxes on inheritances here, in the middle of our conversation. He didn't mention selling off any family treasures, though. Of course, he probably wouldn't take out ads in the papers for it."

"Maybe he was afraid that I'd do that after I talked to his boy Nigel."

"Could be." Bart shoved a hand through his thick hair absently. Tracey smiled when she saw the same lock of hair fall over his lean forehead again despite his gesture. A few things, it seemed, didn't follow their master's dictates.

Bart must have been watching her more closely than she knew. "I'll be damned if I can see anything funny about it," he commented.

"It wasn't that." Tracey tried to think of a plausible explanation without telling the truth, and came up with a lame excuse. "My mind was on something else."

"Then I suggest you move it back to the subject at hand. This is no laughing matter. Unless you've already forgotten—"

"I haven't forgotten anything," she cut in. "But I'd certainly like to. If you must know, I'll be looking over my shoulder for the next two weeks. Either that or go home early."

"There is another alternative." Bart spoke as if choosing his words with care. "You can disappear." As she opened her lips to protest, he overrode her. "Don't start objecting until you hear me out. Right now, Nigel and his chums know you as a redheaded American tourist named Winslow who wanted a bargain in antique tables. I didn't let on that you were a friend of mine when I was talking to Oliver—just a slight acquaintance."

"Which was certainly the truth."

He frowned at her murmured comment but went on without disputing it. "Anyhow, there's no reason for them to connect the two of us. Even if somebody reports our visit to the arcade, there's nothing concrete."

"I still don't see what you're getting at."

"I'm recommending that the redheaded Miss Winslow fold her tent and opt out of the scene. You see those things over there"—he gestured toward a display of wigs on a counter just beyond the coffee-bar entrance. "Take your choice. You can reappear as a blond or a brunette friend of mine. If anyone is curious, I'll tell them that you're from my publisher. I don't care what name you choose." He leaned back as if the problem had been solved. "Want some more coffee?"

"You have to be kidding."

"Well, I know it doesn't taste very good—"

"Not the coffee," she said, and then took an agitated sip as if to prove her point. "I mean the masquerade. Even if I went along with the idea, I couldn't get away with it."

"I don't see why not. Once you cover up that beacon of yours"—he made a negligent gesture toward her flaming hair—"you're halfway home."

His assumption that Tracey possessed little else to commend a second glance didn't escape her. Her lips tightened but she did give the wig counter an appraising glance.

"At least you could try a few on," Bart urged, seeing her indecision. "Who knows, they might bring out all kinds of hidden assets."

Ten minutes later, he nodded approvingly when she was transformed to a pale blond in a collar-length creation of soft waves and casual styling. "That's the best yet," Bart told her. "Maybe a pair of glasses would add a final touch. It's amazing what covering up that red hair does."

Tracey was still undecided. "Well, I think that the people at my hotel will be the only ones confused, and it probably won't faze them. They've seen too many guests wearing wigs. Most women visiting London bring one along—in case they get caught in the rain."

Bart waited until she'd removed it and was shaking out her hair before he signaled the salesgirl to tell her they'd take the wig. It was while they were waiting for it to be packaged that Bart said, "Incidentally, you can forget about your hotel—you won't be staying there. I'll arrange for you to be with me. That's the only way it makes sense," he emphasized. "I told you that Tracey Winslow has to disappear. She checks out of her hotel, and that's it—period."

Tracey ignored the last part of his instructions, fastening instead on the important section. "What do you mean—'with you'?"

He looked disconcerted, but only for an instant. "In my hotel, of course. I'll take care of it."

"You seem to be doing a lot of that. I thought London hotel space was awfully tight."

"They've given me more room than I need. We'll face that when it comes. Right now, let's grab a taxi to your hotel so you can check out. After that, you'll hail another cab, put on the wig, and appear at my hotel as Miss . . ." He paused as he mentally juggled possibilities. "What about 'White' instead of Winslow? That solves the problem of monogrammed luggage."

"I think you're enjoying this. Are you sure you don't write whodunits on the side?"

"No, but maybe I should." He gave the saleslady a careless smile as she delivered the wrapped parcel, and left her staring raptly after him. "Let's get the show started," he said, walking Tracey toward the elevator. "I have an appointment later this afternoon, and I'd rather not miss it."

Tracey didn't bother to subdue her irritation at that offhand remark. "You certainly don't have to as far as I'm concerned. I *have* managed to survive for twenty-three years without your help."

"It might be well if you put a cover on that temper of yours, too. Especially with coexistence in our plans. I'd certainly prefer it." Bart was ostensibly addressing a display mannequin as they waited for the elevator, but Tracey had no doubt about the subject of his remarks.

She maintained a dignified silence as they left the store and he hailed a taxi. Any thoughts she might have had about expressing her disapproval more strongly were stymied when Bart saw her settled into it and then straightened to close the door. "You go ahead to your hotel. I'll trail you in another cab and hang around until you check out. When you get the next cab, it might not hurt to take the long way to my hotel."

"You mean go to Victoria Station as a redhead and come out as a blond?"

"If you like. I'll keep an eye on you as long as it's necessary." He gave her taxi driver a pound note and slammed the door.

Tracey would have liked to ignore his instructions. At least part of them, just so he wouldn't think she made a habit of blind obedience. On the other hand, she was sensible enough to realize that his caution made sense. The memory of that bus bearing down on her and her near-brush with oblivion stayed with her, no matter how much she would have liked to forget it. Someone in the Ardsley House organization had made a mistake when they'd shown her the Regency worktable. The possibility they'd try again to rectify that mistake was enough to cool her anger at Bart's high-handedness.

Before many more minutes had passed on her taxi

ride, she was even grateful that he'd accepted her as a temporary responsibility. It would have been far easier for him to shrug and tell her to look out for herself as he bid her farewell.

That sobering reminder made her follow his instructions to the letter. She went through the formality of checking out, avoiding the urge to look over her shoulder as she moved her baggage to the curb and found another taxi.

She directed that driver to take her to Victoria Station, knowing very well that the traffic congestion around the railroad terminal would serve her purpose nicely. She paid him off there, after instructing him to take her luggage on to Bart's hotel.

Even James Bond would have approved her quick disappearance into the station after that. When she emerged from the women's cloakroom a little later, she was wearing her blond wig and had changed her reversible raincoat from beige to dark green. By then, she was almost enjoying the cloak-and-dagger precautions, even choosing a different exit from the station and picking up a cruising taxi instead of waiting for one in the queue. Once she'd given the driver the name of Bart's hotel in Piccadilly, she sat back and checked the appearance of her wig in her purse mirror. It seemed secure enough, she decided, and thought about putting on her sunglasses to complete the transformation. Since the sun had long since disappeared, she decided that would be definitely gilding the lily. She wanted to slip unobtrusively into Bart's hotel—not arrive like a fugitive Hollywood starlet.

It wasn't until she'd paid off the taxi and assured the hotel doorman that her luggage had already arrived that she started having misgivings. Did she sit in the lobby and wait, or was she supposed to march up to that imposing reception desk and tell the clerk that Mr. Jennings had reserved a room for her? The name was . . . Her hand went to her lips as panic struck. What in God's name *was* her name?

Fortunately the reply came as she was decanted from the revolving door into the marble foyer.

"Ah, Miss White—I'm glad that you arrived safely. Welcome to London!" Bart was hovering by the hall porter's desk, ostensibly reading a weekly guide for activities in the city. He replaced it in the rack as he came forward to shake hands. "I've already registered for you," he said loudly, drawing her on to the bank of elevators beyond the lounge. "You're doing fine," he added in a quiet tone once they were beyond the reception desk and hall porter's bailiwick. "They want your passport number, but we can furnish it later."

"The passport number isn't for anybody named White," she reminded him.

He shrugged. "I know, but it's just a formality, and by the time anybody questions it, we'll be long gone. Besides, there's no law against traveling incognito. They probably have some suspicions about you already."

She pulled up a few steps from the elevator. "What do you mean by that?"

"Simply that there weren't any single rooms, so they booked you into the second bedroom in my suite. It's no trouble—it wasn't being used anyway," he added quickly when a frown marred her forehead. "They may suspect that we have more than a working relationship—"

"Now look here, I'm not going to—"

"—so they'll be surprised to find that both bedrooms have been occupied in the morning," he continued implacably. "Serve them right for having warped minds in the first place."

"Well, if you're sure," Tracey yielded, reassured by his words. "What about my bags?"

"They're stored in the porter's room, but I'll arrange to have them sent up right away. You take this room key and go on ahead. I'll be up as soon as I've taken care of things here. Incidentally, I'll have some tea sent up, as well. You look as if you could use it."

"Do you ever let anybody get a word in edgeways?" she protested, starting to laugh in spite of herself.

"Just occasionally—and never on Mondays." He grinned and was starting to walk away when he pulled up abruptly. "Damn! Stella would be early."

He turned back again, to find Tracey still standing where he'd left her, utterly confused by his words. Comprehension came when she recognized the tall blond woman she'd met before as she waved and walked down the corridor toward them.

Behind Tracey, there came the sound of elevator doors opening and a respectful male voice inquiring, "Going up?"

"This lady is—to the fourth floor. Just wait a minute," Bart replied. Then, without another word, he pulled Tracey into his arms. He ignored her faint gasp of surprise, smothering it effectively as he covered her lips with his.

The kiss was an expert sensual onslaught and it wasn't one bit less effective because it was calculated and deliberate. Tracey was only aware that his mouth was cool and firm and that it seemed like an eternity before she was allowed to surface dazedly from his embrace.

Even then, Bart didn't give her a chance to say anything, simply handing her into the elevator and jerking his head to the operator in unspoken command.

The doors started closing while she was still leaning against the gilt walls, trying to get her breathing back on a regular cycle. Her tremulous expression wouldn't have left Bart in any doubt of her feelings if he'd been looking at her; instead he had turned and was greeting Stella Frome, whose patrician features mirrored incredulity and pique in equal measure.

"You *did* want four, miss?"

The words seemed to come from a long way away. Tracey blinked and discovered that the elevator doors had closed and opened again. This time, to a blessedly empty corridor. "Yes, thanks." She looked around the elevator, trying to remember if she had any luggage with her.

"Do you need any assistance?" The elderly operator was watching her in some concern.

She got a grip on herself and shook her head, stepping out into the hallway with her room key in hand. "No, thank you. I'm just fine."

The doors had closed again before she managed to focus on the key long enough to decipher the room number, and she walked slowly down the corridor, checking the doors.

When she finally discovered the right one, she unlocked it and poked her head around the jamb to survey the empty sitting room it disclosed.

She lingered on the threshold long enough to note

the stiff upholstered furniture and a small bar in the corner next to a built-in television cabinet before moving across to check the adjoining room on the right. It turned out to be a well-furnished bedroom where two leather suitcases rested on luggage racks at the foot of a big double bed. An open door on the far wall showed a gleaming tile bathroom.

Tracey's eyes narrowed and she turned back across the sitting room to check out the remaining door on the other side. This time, it was a smaller bedroom and bath. There was only a view of the interior courtyard from the satin-draped window, but that was the least of her concerns. The room was unoccupied—everything confirmed it, from the carefully arranged magazines on the glass-topped dressing table to the packets of foam bath gel on a shelf in the bathroom.

Tracey let out a sigh of relief and went back to the door which connected with the sitting room. She closed it firmly and turned the key in the lock. Only after that did she sink on the edge of the bed and stare down at the pearl-gray carpet beneath her feet. It, at least, stayed obligingly in place. It was a relief, because in the last five minutes everything else seemed to have suddenly spun into a different sequence—like a slot machine in Las Vegas.

She linked her fingers in her lap, trying to still their trembling as she thought about it. It would be nice if she could dwell on winning the jackpot. But jackpots were for women like Stella Frome, and Tracey wasn't so bemused that she didn't know it.

It occurred to her suddenly that she might have walked into a more frightening situation than the one she thought she was avoiding. Certainly she'd have to follow her own instincts from now on and not rely on Bart Jennings for anything.

For, without a doubt, he could turn out to be her most dangerous threat of all.

5

Tracey stayed where she was until a knock sounded on the door which led directly to the hallway. "Room service" came a muffled voice as she got up to answer the summons.

"But I didn't order anything," she said, opening the door.

An elderly waiter started to wheel in the cart. "Mr. Jennings ordered the tea for you, miss," he said with a quick look at the slip in his hand. "Where would you like it?"

"Well, in here, I guess."

"I can serve it in the sitting room if you'd prefer."

"No, thank you." Tracey wasn't in any doubt about that. The last thing she wanted was to be sitting in the other room if Bart and Stella came upstairs.

The same apprehension kept her from changing her clothes or unpacking her suitcases, which arrived while she sipped the tea. However, it didn't keep her from eating the wafer-thin cucumber sandwiches that were on a plate next to the teapot. She looked yearningly at the decorated fruitcake on another plate and shook her head. After what had happened, she shouldn't be increasing her debt to Bart. At least until he offered a reasonable explanation for his parting gesture.

Not that Bart Jennings was the type to give explanations; he was far more apt to put her on the defensive as soon as he appeared. It would have been interesting, though, to know what he'd told Stella Frome as soon as the elevator doors had closed.

Tracey managed to waste a little more time by drinking a second cup of tea, but finally she pushed the tea cart out into the corridor and came back into the bedroom.

Finally she checked to make sure the doors were locked before unpacking a robe from her suitcase. It was ridiculous to sit around like a ventriloquist's dummy waiting for someone to pull the strings. She tugged off her wig with a decisive gesture and headed for the bathroom. The one thing she wanted just then was a shower and a chance to shampoo her hair. Amazing how good it felt to be able to run her fingers through it without sneaking a glance in the mirror to make sure that her blond coiffure was still squarely on her head.

The hot shower felt wonderful, and she used a towel from the heated rack as a turban for her wet hair. She dried herself with another and was just pulling on an ivory-colored robe with print flowers blooming around the hem when a knock sounded. This time it was on her bedroom door which led to the sitting room.

Her hand stilled from tying a bow at the gathered neckline of her robe. "Who is it?"

"Now, who do you think?" came a familiar masculine voice. "Come on out—I want to talk to you."

It certainly wasn't an apologetic tone and it was an

order, not a request. "I'm not dressed," she countered, wishing that he'd given her another half-hour to look decent. The robe was all right, but a white towel turban didn't do much for feminine glamour.

"Well, put a robe on. You must have one. If you don't, grab a blanket. Hurry up, will you? I don't have that much time."

His comment made Tracey so annoyed that she forgot her reluctance. "I'd hate to keep you waiting," she snarled as she stalked over and unlocked the door. "I didn't know that I was expected to . . ." Her diatribe stopped abruptly when she noted his impressive appearance.

Sometime in the interval, he'd changed from sport coat and slacks into a well-tailored dinner jacket. Her gaze took in the pleated shirt, classic black tie, and dark trousers with a knife crease. How had she ever thought that Bart Jennings existed in rumpled tweeds?

"Expected to what?" he countered when her glance met his again.

"It wasn't important," she said, feeling more ill-at-ease than ever. She needed a ball gown and diamonds to even operate in the same league. Her robe might be acceptable, but the towel on her head was slipping and she had to put up a hand to save it. "I just washed my hair," she managed feebly.

A fleeting look of amusement softened his mouth. "Which one?"

"What do you mean?"

"Which set of hair?"

Her lips tightened. "My own, naturally."

"I wasn't sure. Why bother with that thing, then?" He reached over and plucked off the towel, tossing it over the bedroom doorknob. "I've seen wet hair before, but I wasn't sure what happened to a wet wig."

"Honestly!" Tracey drew herself up to her full height. "Either you've written too damned many swashbucklers or you're starting to believe your publicity." She ran a distracted hand through her still-damp hair. "I haven't even had a chance to comb it."

"I hadn't noticed. Go ahead if it makes you feel better," he said magnanimously, and gestured her back into the bedroom.

Tracey hesitated and then walked over to the dressing table, trying not to panic when he came in and sat down, propping himself against her headboard to watch.

He was ostensibly relaxed, but Tracey felt his latent strength even from across the room. She tried to avoid his glance in the mirror after that. Finally she was driven to ask, "Haven't you anything else to do?"

"Unfortunately, yes," he said, overlooking her annoyance and sticking to the literal meaning. "That's what I wanted to tell you. I'm sorry about deserting you tonight, but Stella had set up this theater date earlier in the week."

"Really, you don't have to explain."

"I wish you'd let me finish," he cut in, stopping her objections like a hot knife going through butter. "Damned if I see how Oscar gets any points across if you interrupt him every third word."

"I don't see what my boss has to do with it. There's no similarity at all. He doesn't go around installing me in hotel rooms and . . ." She broke off as she realized where her hasty words were leading.

"He doesn't kiss you in hotel lobbies," Bart had no

trouble finishing the sentence. "Was that next on your list?"

"That's right." She put her comb down with leashed violence and swung round on the dressing-table bench to face him. "You might have warned me that you wanted to make Miss Frome jealous." As he only frowned in response, she added impatiently, "You'll have to find somebody else for your games next time. I don't want to get involved."

He folded his arms over his immaculate shirtfront. "It was just a kiss—not attempted rape. There's no need to chew the scenery over it."

"I *knew* I'd end up on the defensive." Tracey was so annoyed that her voice cracked. "Is it too much to hope for an apology, or are they only for ordinary mortals?"

"If you don't simmer down, I'll turn you over my knee. Then you'll *really* have something to complain about." He sat up and shoved one of her pillows behind his back. "Why in hell should I apologize for one kiss? We're both consenting adults—although you're hardly acting like one at the moment."

She gestured with open palms. "That's not the point. You can't go around kissing one woman because you want to make another one jealous. That *was* the reason, I presume."

"I didn't write a scenario ahead of time," he countered, meeting her sarcasm head-on. "You could call it a contributing factor. Stella has a tendency to get a little overpowering—" He frowned as Tracey gave an audible snort. "If we could discuss things on an adult level, it would be easier."

"I'll try to cope," she said sweetly.

He ignored that. "I would have tried to get another ticket for tonight, but it seemed safer to keep it a threesome. Stella's asked another man, too. She believes in having two strings to her bow whenever possible." Bart stood up then and wandered over to the dressing table, picking up Tracey's perfume atomizer and sniffing it absently. "Nice. What's it called?"

His question caught her off-guard. "Calèche," she said. "I hope to buy some more if I get back to Paris."

"Better discard the blond wig if you do. That fragrance belongs to a redhead." His glance raked her jersey robe, not missing a curve on the way. "That outfit doesn't look very warm."

"I was just about to get dressed. You didn't give me time."

"I wasn't complaining." The devilment in his eyes showed that he'd discovered that she wasn't wearing anything under the robe long before her explanation. "You'd better get another towel and dry your hair, though, or you'll end up in a pneumonia ward."

She turned back and picked up her comb again to cover her confusion. While she had no intention of allowing any more passes on Bart's part, he didn't have to sound like some professor lecturing on a healthy body. "I'm not a bit cold," she lied determinedly.

"In that case, I won't ask the porter to send up a portable heater for this bedroom. The British turn off their central heating in June, no matter what the temperature." He got to his feet. "I'd better be going, or Stella will start tracking me down."

"Yes, of course." Tracey tried to sound as if she didn't mind sitting alone in a chilly hotel room, destined for another riotous night of British television. "I hope you have a good time."

Her bleak tone must have gotten through to Bart, because he frowned as he paused by the hall door. "It's a damned shame that you'll be stuck up here for dinner, but there's no sense in your taking chances in the lobby. Even if Oliver's with us, you can't be too careful."

"Oliver?"

"Oliver Rustad. I told you Stella had invited him to the theater tonight. That's why you'd better stay undercover. Stella would probably see through your disguise if she spends much time with you, and I don't want her tipping our hand to Oliver. Not when I'm angling for an invitation to visit Ardsley House." Bart made it sound as if he'd gone over it a hundred times before. "Why are you looking at me that way?"

"Because I'd like to hit you over the head with this ashtray. That's why." She hefted a heavy crystal one from the dressing table. "I would, if I could afford to replace it."

"The head or the ashtray?" he asked wickedly. "Put it down, you idiot—I'm just kidding. What are you mad about now?"

"Because you didn't tell me that Stella had invited Oliver Rustad. You just mentioned another man."

"No wonder you were sizzling under that robe and didn't mind the temperature. I'll tell you what happens when I get back." He gave her a careless pat on the nearest part of her anatomy, which turned out to be her derriere. Then he reached over and plucked the ashtray from her hand, putting it back on the dressing table. "You won't have to defend your virtue this time."

"Can I count on that?" she asked, stepping pointedly out of his reach.

His amusement faded. "I think, Miss Winslow, that you read the wrong kind of books."

"You're right. Tomorrow I'm going to pick up one on beginning karate. Enjoy your evening."

"Thanks. I'll be sure not to disturb you when I come in, so you won't have to leave a candle in the window."

"Or a chair under the doorknob?" she confirmed. "There's just one other thing. Are you going to try to arrange for Miss White to spend the weekend at Ardsley House, too?"

He paused, halfway into the hall. "Miss White?"

"Me," she said with terrible patience. "Your secretary or editor or whatever I am."

"Publishing associate," he replied smoothly. "And, no, I'm not. You'll be safer out of range here in London. You don't have to worry about your story—I'll be glad to hand the facts over when I come back. If there's anything worth printing. And you'd better dig out some flannel pajamas," he added as a kindly note before closing the door. "You're starting to turn blue."

Tracey wished that she was still holding the ashtray. Instead, she had to settle for slamming her comb down on the end of the mauve bedspread. Turning blue, was she! Well, she might be, but temperature had nothing to do with it! At least, not much, she amended, digging a sweater out of her suitcase and pulling it on over her thin robe. If Bart thought she was going to be left parked in London while he larked around the south coast of England researching her story, he had leaks in his attic. She took a deep breath of satisfaction, which changed into a sneeze halfway through.

That made her resolve to be sensible. She walked into the sitting room and dried her hair next to the heater. After that she put on a pair of warm slacks and a sweater before ordering her dinner from room service.

The steak-and-mushroom pie was delicious, and any other time she would have accorded it her full attention. Just then, however, she was deciding what kind of an explanation she would leave for Bart when she checked out the next morning. It might be the cowardly way to handle things, but it would save a monumental argument.

In the end, she wrote a note that was remarkable for evasiveness and brevity:

Dear Bart,

After thinking it over, I decided to go and re-search the story myself. I'll drop you a note and let you know how things turn out.

Sincerely,
Tracey

P.S. Thank you for rescuing me today. I promise to be more careful after this.

The last sentence was added impulsively—not that it would make him any happier, but it might soothe his commendable sense of responsibility. She bit her lip as she read over the note again and then slipped it into an envelope before she could change her mind.

After that, she didn't let herself think about what the future might bring for them. If she faced facts, there wasn't any future at all. She'd been at a disadvantage from the start, since Bart was just being polite to a protégé of Oscar's. He'd pulled her out of danger, mopped her face, and fed her lunch as any friend might do. Transferring her to his hotel later had certainly been beyond the call of duty. Maybe that was why he felt entitled to that kiss in front of the elevators; it was a small price for her to pay, and if it worked the miracle for him with the beautiful Stella, then no harm was done.

She thought of all those things as she watched a dull program on the training of lifeboat crews and a preview of European soccer. When the news came on, she changed into pajamas and brushed her teeth. The weatherman promised rain for Scotland, Ireland, and most of England, waving his wand over the south coast as he spoke.

Tracey sighed and left her raincoat out of her suitcase. Then she carefully set her travel alarm for six and put it on the bed table next to her pillow. She put the note and envelope with Bart's name on it right next to the clock. There'd be time to slip that under his bedroom door in the morning. She certainly didn't want to run the risk of leaving it in the sitting room, where he might see it when he came in later. Always supposing that he did come back to the hotel after his date.

Her lips thinned as she thought about that possibility. The way he'd kissed her showed that he'd had a great deal of practice in such things, and the casual smack he'd later administered on her derriere displayed his consummate ease with the feminine sex. She had no doubt that he could write a best-seller on

"How to Deal with Women" if he ever gave up historical sagas. He would, however, have to find another body to practice on.

Tracey closed the door which separated her bedroom from the sitting room and slid the bolt on her side. She lay awake in bed for a half-hour, tossing restlessly on the mattress. It wasn't surprising that Bart didn't return in the interval, Tracey told herself. Miracles didn't come by the score, and she'd had more than her share for one day. On that sobering conclusion, she finally closed her eyes.

6

She slept lightly, waking several times before the alarm finally erupted by her ear. Her arm went out to quash the lever a split second later. After that, she remained motionless, making sure that there was no noise beyond her bedroom door to show that Bart had heard the alarm. Providing he was in the other bedroom at all.

Unfortunately there was no way Tracey could check that without tiptoeing across and opening his door—something to be avoided at all costs.

The continued silence in the suite reassured her, and her heartbeat settled back to its normal cadence. She yawned as she got quietly out of bed and walked over to twitch aside the heavy satin draw drapery on the window.

The weatherman had been right in his forecast; it was another gray, overcast morning. At least the English wouldn't have to worry about a drought, she thought wryly as she tiptoed into the bathroom and closed the door.

Tracey made do with a sponge bath rather than risk the noise of the shower. Afterward she didn't waste any time donning a peacock-blue dress with mohair collar and cuffs. It was comfortable for travel and warm enough that she could manage with just a raincoat over it.

Five minutes later, she was moving her suitcases out in the deserted hall corridor, making two trips so that she wouldn't bump the door and disturb Bart.

She took a final look around her bedroom before putting on her raincoat. Her last action was to walk silently across the sitting room and shove the envelope with her note under his bedroom door.

She moved on out to the hall after that. It was ridiculous to feel sad and guilty about her actions—as if she was casting off from a safe haven to venture into the unknown. Then she remembered Bart's decision to handle the Ardsley House matter by himself, and her chin firmed. While she waited for the elevator doors to open, her glance strayed to a nearby mirror and she almost did a double-take on seeing a blond woman staring back at her. That damned wig! For a moment she'd forgotten she was wearing it, but since she'd checked in the hotel as a blond, it would be best to check out the same way.

The hall porter on duty in the lobby was horrified that she hadn't called for help with her bags.

By then Tracey was happy to have his assistance and turned them over to him gratefully. "If you could get a cab for me, I'd appreciate it," she suggested before going across to the cashier's desk.

"I'll notify the doorman, miss," the porter informed her, letting her know that protocol would be followed, despite the early hour.

The cashier was a middle-aged woman who put down her cup of tea hastily when Tracey approached the grilled window.

"You're checking out, Miss White?" she asked, as if needing confirmation.

"Yes, please," Tracey replied.

The cashier had found the record by then. "But Mr. Jennings said you'd be staying for several days. Is he checking out, too?"

"I don't know. He was still sleeping when I left," Tracey said, and then felt her ears grow red.

"I see." There was a great deal of British understatement in the two words.

"Anyhow, I'd like to pay my bill, please," Tracey said stiffly. "If you'd just tell me what I owe."

"The account has already been taken care of, Miss White. Mr. Jennings was most explicit about that. Unless he's changed his mind . . ." Her hand went out to the phone. "I'll just call and find out."

"No—don't do that!" Tracey commanded, making the cashier jerk her hand back from the receiver. "He'd be terribly upset," Tracey went on, trying to smooth things over. "It was late when he got in and he didn't want to be disturbed this morning."

"Then there's nothing I can do," the woman said, drawing herself up and sounding official. "Not without proper authorization. Our Mr. Philbrick won't be in for another hour."

"Who's he?"

"The day manager, madam. He can take care of the matter."

"No, thanks." Tracey sounded just as definite. "I'll settle the account with Mr. Jennings when I see him again."

"I'm sure that would be the easiest way." The older woman's tone was kind, but it showed that the kind of payment she envisaged didn't involve writing checks.

Tracey's already hot cheeks grew redder still. Probably she was imagining things, she told herself as she zipped her purse and thanked the cashier. It was simply that she was out of her field and didn't know the rules for a one-night stand.

She could hear the doorman's whistle still shrilling for a taxi in the quiet streets, so she occupied herself with a pile of tourist pamphlets from the hall porter's counter while she waited. There was a brochure on Stately Homes which she tucked in the side of her purse along with one extolling the scenic glories of England's south coast. "It's all right to take these, isn't it?" she asked.

"Certainly, miss. Take as many as you like." The uniformed porter switched his glance to the entrance. "I believe that's your taxi now."

Tracey moved with him to the revolving door and tipped him as she went out. "Thank you, you've been very kind."

"My pleasure. Come back again, Miss White."

The doorman was equally gracious and obliging, making sure her bags were stored alongside the taxi driver before asking, "Where to, miss?"

"Waterloo, please."

It wasn't until Tracey was seated and the taxi was under way that she wished she hadn't made her destination quite so obvious. Then she shook her head, dismissing any ideas that Bart would be interested enough in her departure to ask questions.

Fortunately there was a vacant luggage cart when the cab arrived at Waterloo a little later, and she piled her suitcases on it. She wheeled the cart into the old railroad station and checked the train-departure board without finding the information she wanted. Only after conferring with the man at a ticket window did she discover that the next train for Southhampton left in forty minutes. At least that meant there'd be time for her to get a token breakfast in the station. It was a welcome prospect, since she didn't know whether there'd be any food available on the two-hour journey and her stomach was already protesting its empty state.

The railroad buffet had a few bleary-eyed souls leaning against stand-up counters, since it was still too early for the commuter rush. Tracey wheeled her luggage over to survey the offerings in refrigerated glass displays and then, in dismay, read the menu printed above them.

It wasn't fair, she thought, giving the food another look. According to British Rail, breakfast commuters were expected to choose between a plastic-wrapped Sardine Super or a Salami-Salad sandwich. Even at high noon, the selection wouldn't have thrilled anybody. At breakfast, it was beyond comprehension.

"Coffee, miss?" asked an attendant, watching Tracey's disappointed face.

"Yes, thanks. Is that all there is?" Tracey gestured toward the case.

"Unless you want a biscuit." The woman pulled a cardboard box of packaged cookies from beneath the counter. "There are some plain ones in there. White or black?"

"I beg your pardon?"

"The coffee. White or black?"

"Oh, white, please. And a package of the plain ones."

Once the transaction was completed, Tracey moved across to a stand-up counter to eat her Spartan repast. Life in Britain was a feast or a famine, she decided. When she was alone, it was no trouble keeping her waistline within bounds. That's why it had been such a treat to have Bart plying her with calories the day before. Well, he wouldn't be offering her hospitality again. Not after discovering that she'd done a bunk from the hotel. For an instant, she wondered if he might be already trying to track her down, and then she grimaced. It was more likely that he'd be calling room service for champagne to celebrate. And when he saw the gorgeous Stella or Oliver the next time, he could truthfully say that his "editorial assistant" had gone on her way.

A particularly pungent smell roused Tracey from her reverie, and she discovered that another early traveler was unwrapping a Sardine Super at her elbow with every evidence of delight.

She made her empty coffeecup an excuse for a hasty withdrawal and left the man to his fish course. It was still too early for boarding the train, so she passed her time reading notices on the various bulletin boards. They ranged from "Please support a coffee morning and a 'bring and buy' " to "Enjoy the take-away bar at the station buffet." The last made her utter an unladylike snort, and she wheeled her luggage past the station flower shop to read the book titles at the newsagents. She paid for a morning paper to take on the train and then noticed with relief that the stationmaster was putting up the notice for the Southampton train.

There wasn't any crowd at the gate, since commuters were pouring into the city for work rather than heading the other way. Tracey had her choice of compartments in a car near the end of the train. An obliging porter who was walking by helped her to get her heavy suitcases aboard and wished her a pleasant trip as he closed the door.

In the few minutes before the train left Waterloo, she stayed away from the window, occupying a seat next to the corridor. When the engine pulled out of the station exactly on time, she let out a slight sigh. It was relief, she told herself. Of course it was.

Rather than dwell on it, she unfolded her morning paper and immersed herself in the headlines. The conductor came through to check her rail pass just after they'd left the outskirts of the city, and he was closely followed by a white-uniformed dining-car employee pushing a shopping cart full of sandwiches and urns with coffee and tea.

Tracey bought another cup of coffee and shook her head at his offer of cheese-and-tomato sandwiches. Southampton was only two hours away and she could always order a late breakfast at the hotel. It would have been better if she'd phoned ahead for a room reservation, but she hadn't wanted to ask the hall porter at Bart's hotel to do it, and the vagaries of British public telephones had deterred her at Waterloo.

"It's all right," she muttered under her breath. "I'll start with the hotels and work my way down to bed-and-breakfast, if I have to. There's bound to be a room somewhere."

Such a logical approach made her feel better about the prospect. So did her second cup of coffee. The green fields and hedgerows of the countryside flashed by, interrupted only by picturesque English villages where they hadn't changed a building in the last hundred years. Tracey relaxed under their spell and concentrated on the letter she'd write to Bart when she'd finally brought the Ardsley House story to a triumphant conclusion.

About then, she decided that perhaps she would

do better to arrive at Southampton as a blond, after all. If her suspicions about the estate had any validity, it would be better to keep her red hair hidden while in the neighborhood. Especially if Nigel Pelham or the man from the Piccadilly flea market had described her appearance, there was no point in taking chances.

Tracey started hauling down her suitcases from the upper rack of the compartment about five minutes before the scheduled arrival time at Southampton. Almost simultaneously the speed of the train lessened as the main track went across a network of connecting spur lines. Tracey peered through the window and discovered that they were near the long stretch of docks for which Southampton was famed. Even before the *Mayflower* had sailed for Plymouth and New England, she knew that Britons had used The Solent and Southampton Water as their shipping center. From the number of loading cranes and warehouses on view, the port was still growing. A fleeting glimpse of a cruise ship outward-bound toward the Isle of Wight brought a touch of yearning for an instant before she dismissed it. Her budget scarcely stretched to excursion air fare at that moment—cruises were strictly in the "someday" category.

The train ground to a halt at a station which held little of the bustle of Waterloo. Tracey struggled onto the platform with her bags and saw with relief that the exit for taxis wasn't far away.

By the time she reached it, there was only one car left and the driver of it was half-hidden behind a newspaper. She had to put her bags down on the curb and open the rear door of the small car before his head came over the front page.

"Sorry, miss," he said, folding the paper and putting it down at his side. "Needing a taxi, were you?"

"And a hotel," Tracey agreed. She was relieved to see that he looked like an amiable soul as he slid out from under the wheel to reach for her luggage. "I haven't made a reservation—could you recommend one?"

"Want to be downtown, did you?"

"I guess so. At least it would be easier until I can rent a car." A sudden thought struck her. "Unless there's a hotel near Ardsley House."

His stocky figure straightened from putting her bags in the trunk. "Lord love us! Are you answering one of Aunt Phoebe's advertisements?" Tracey's perplexed look made him reach in the front seat for his paper and open it to the classified section. "Right here," he said, and pointed as he read, " 'Temporary female help needed to assist with banquet facilities and upkeep at Hampshire estate. Experienced domestic service preferred. Apply to housekeeper, Ardsley House.' " He turned back to Tracey and explained, "Auntie's the housekeeper there and she was telling my mum just last night that they're having a shocking time getting decent help. 'Course, the wages aren't much," he added truthfully.

Tracey, who had been thinking fast, said hastily, "That's all right. Money doesn't matter." The young driver's reaction to that statement made her hastily alter it. "Right now, I'm just looking for a stopgap. It's hard for a tourist to get work—you know, permits and things like that."

He shook his head. "I don't think Aunt Phoebe would want to get mucked up with a lot of red tape. And Mr. Rustad wouldn't approve of anything illegal."

"Mr. Rustad?" Tracey tried to sound as if she'd never heard the name before.

"He owns Ardsley—but he's not there very often. I understand he's having trouble keeping the place up these days—that's why he's trying medieval banquets now. He's signed on with some tour agencies this summer, too."

"Then I should think your aunt would be glad to see another job applicant. Look, maybe you could phone and see if there's any place going. I promise that there won't be any trouble—I'd just like to work for a night or so and make some extra money. If she needs me right away, I could report after I check in at a hotel. That is, if you could drive me there."

He pulled his ear thoughtfully and then nodded. "Right. There's a phone around the corner. I'll tell her about you but not supply any extra information. There'll be time for that once you collect a pay packet."

"Wonderful! Let me give you some change for the telephone," Tracey said as he started toward the station concourse.

"I'll add it to your fare," he said genially over his shoulder, and disappeared around the corner.

Tracy was waiting in the backseat of the small car when he reappeared five minutes later. He made a thumbs-up signal before he slid behind the steering wheel. "Everything's on. Aunt Phoebe's so glad that she won't have to carry soup bowls herself, she practically fell on my neck over the phone. I told her you had to find a place to stay but you'd be up to see her later this afternoon. Just for a look round the place," he added as he started the car. "You can work the banquet tomorrow night."

"That sounds perfect." She caught his glance in

the rearview mirror as he drove out of the station lot. "Now, if my luck holds with a hotel—everything will be perfect. You *did* say you could recommend one, didn't you?" she persisted as she saw a frown go over his face.

"The Poseidon is a bit pricey, but it's the best location."

"It doesn't matter now that I have a chance for a job. The extra money coming in should tide me over nicely." Then she added, "I hope this Poseidon will have room."

He grinned companionably. "It happens I have a cousin who works in the kitchen. Besides, there's no trouble getting a room unless a cruise ship is in port."

"That's a relief." She stared with interest as he skirted the edge of what appeared to be the town Common—a parklike section edged with shade trees. People of all ages were strolling the paths or just sitting on benches enjoying the quiet oasis next to the bustling city center.

"The hotel's just past there." Her driver gestured ahead of them to a substantial brick building almost on the edge of the Common. "If you don't like the food in the dining room, there's an Italian restaurant a block away. I could take you tonight unless there's some bloke of yours who might object." He eyed her speculatively as he slowed to pull into the drive of the hotel.

Tracey improvised, not wanting to get involved. "I'm sorry—there *is* somebody."

"I thought there might be." He sounded resigned as he braked. "No matter, it was worth a try. You go in and register while I bring your cases. Tell them Ian brought you, if there's any bother."

Tracey nodded and pushed through the hotel's revolving door. The medium-size lobby was plainly furnished with a grouping of upholstered furniture in the center, a hall porter's counter to the left, and an elevator to her right. A harassed woman of middle age was behind the reception desk, but she moved over to work an old-fashioned switchboard as Tracey approached.

She handled the plug board with some annoyance and said, "Sorry to keep you waiting, miss—this morning I'm doing everybody's work," when she walked back to the counter. As Ian came through the entrance laden with bags, she frowned at him and raised her eyebrows at Tracey. "Are you staying with us, then?"

"I hope so. A single room if you have one."

"How long will you be needing it?"

"Probably three or four days. I'm not sure of my plans." Tracey realized she'd made a mistake as soon as the words were out, because the clerk's frown deepened as she stared across the counter. Apparently any hotel guest who didn't have a definite itinerary might be tempted to blow the office safe or snatch the silver. "Actually, I'm waiting for a confirmation from my travel agent," Tracey added, hoping that sounded better.

The woman's expression relaxed somewhat. "I see. Well, we would appreciate it if you'd let us know your plans as soon as you can. May I have your name, please?"

"Winslow," Tracey said, aware that she'd have to present her passport to fill out the registration card. Fortunately Ian had unloaded her bags by the porter's desk and had lingered there to talk with the elderly uniformed man. Since Tracey hadn't planned to use her own name when applying at Ardsley House, it was getting more complicated than she'd anticipated.

The clerk nodded absently and pulled out a card for her to sign. "Fortunately, we're not crowded this week." She went on to quote a rate which was considerably less than Tracey had been paying in London. When that was agreed on, the woman banged a bell near the switchboard, making the porter who'd been talking to Ian look over with a frown.

"It's all right. I'm not in any hurry," Tracey said hastily, and took her room key from the counter where the clerk had pointedly placed it. "As a matter of fact, I want to arrange for a tour with the taxi driver." She moved hastily away from the desk and intercepted Ian just as he was coming across the room.

"Everything settled?" he wanted to know.

"Yes, thanks." She led him back toward the entrance. "Is it convenient for you to drive me out to Ardsley this afternoon?"

He nodded briskly. "I go off duty at five. If I pick you up at three, you'll have plenty of time to settle things at Ardsley. I can even include a scenic loop of the New Forest on the way. It's one of the things to see in this part of the country and only costs a little extra."

"That sounds fine," she assured him. "I'll be outside and waiting at three."

"There's no need. I can phone up to your room—except that I don't know your name," he said, remembering.

"It's Tracey." Before he could question her further, she smiled and added, "I'll be ready and waiting down here. I'd hate to miss this chance of a job."

"Whatever you say." He gave her a casual salute and nodded to the porter, who by then had loaded her bags on a cart and was patiently standing by the elevator.

Tracey lingered to watch Ian go through the door before she walked back across the lobby. "I'm sorry to keep you waiting," she told the older man.

"No trouble, miss. There's plenty of time," he said, directing a defiant glance toward the dragon behind the reception desk before he gestured Tracey into the elevator.

Her hotel room was almost Spartan in its furnishings, but immaculately clean, and boasted an electric kettle plus the furnishings of a tea tray at one end of the dressing table.

Before he disappeared, the porter told her that lunch was served only in the hotel bar. "Dinner's served in the dining room, though," he went on proudly. "Mind you, it's best to make a reservation to be sure of a table. This is a busy place at night."

Tracey was surprised to hear it, since her initial impression of the hotel was that any woman wanting to play "Sleeping Beauty" would have a long wait for a prince under eighty to appear. She didn't let her feelings show as she said meekly, "I'll try to remember."

That seemed to satisfy him, and he gave a grudging nod of approval before closing the door behind him.

Tracey didn't waste any time in checking her wig, making sure that it was still properly adjusted. Somehow it didn't seem so bad to stay in her new role since she had a chance to work at Ardsley House. There'd be plenty of time to scout the premises, and actually working there would be infinitely better than just touring the place in a group.

The thought of tour groups made her frown suddenly as she remembered Bart's desire to wangle an overnight invitation. Then she shrugged and picked up her key from the top of the bureau. From all accounts, the estate must occupy plenty of acreage and the chances of running into him were practically nil.

Tracey was still cheered by that thought as she went back down to the lobby, this time turning into the short hallway which led to the bar.

A murmur of voices spilled out of the room, but it didn't prepare her for the jam of humanity crowding the premises when she crossed the threshold. Apparently all of the hotel's guests plus a good number of locals had chosen it as the place to either eat or drink their lunch. There weren't many of the former lined up in front of a buffet table, where alcohol lamps kept the contents of a big chafing dish warm. The rest of the table boasted a platter of sausage rolls, a round watery-looking quiche, plus a cheese board with apples and oranges around it.

Tracey surveyed the items without too much enthusiasm, noting that patrons helped themselves until the harried waiter in charge eventually caught up with them to present a bill.

She turned then to see if there was a place to sit before she filled a plate. At first glance it appeared all of the chairs and windowsills were occupied except for a place next to an elderly lady who was sitting in a far corner. An equally elderly cocker spaniel was sleeping at her feet, apparently oblivious of the commotion around him.

Tracey grinned and decided she could have worse companions. As her glance swept casually over the rest of the room, it stopped abruptly on the young man sitting at the end of the bar. He was smoothing his mustache and absently glanced into the mirror behind the bar to intercept Tracey's startled stare. For an instant Nigel Pelham treated her to a masculine appraisal which was meant to be flattering but made Tracey drop her eyes. Before he was tempted to do more, she hurried over to the old lady in the corner, who was sipping sherry with every evidence of enjoyment.

Tracey sat down on a stool at her side. "I hope you aren't saving this for anyone," she said breathlessly, trusting that Nigel would think she was greeting an old friend if he was still watching. "I wanted to have a bite of lunch but it's too crowded by the buffet table."

"It's easier to get a drink," the woman agreed calmly. She raised a gnarled hand to attract the waiter's attention on the first try. "Now then dear, what would you like?" she asked, turning to Tracey. "They stock a nice sherry."

"That will be fine. Er—can I order another for you?" Tracey saw that Nigel had resumed his conversation with the man beside him at the bar but was idly observing her as he spoke.

"No, thank you, love. If I had more than one—Ferdie would have to lead me home and the poor chap isn't up to it."

"If you're sure." Tracey didn't know who Ferdie was but it seemed safer to agree. She waited until the waiter had taken her order and threaded his way through the tables back to the bar before asking, "Were you saving this stool for your friend? I'll be glad to move when he comes."

The woman leaned down to place an affectionate

hand on the old spaniel's head. "This is Ferdie. Nobody objects to him on the floor, but it might be a bit much if he started coming up in the world. Isn't that right, boy?"

The spaniel sighed as he moved his head slightly on her worn oxfords, stretching out his muzzle so that his chin rested on the edge of the carpet as well.

"He's beautifully behaved." Tracey forgot her problems long enough to bend over and pat the dog's back. "How old is he?"

"Almost fourteen." The woman broke off when the waiter brought Tracey's sherry and nodded in satisfaction as he deposited a small bowl of nuts alongside. When he'd been paid and gone on his way, the woman raised her glass in a toast. "Your health, dear. Are you over from the States?"

Tracey almost choked on her wine, and then remembered that the taxi driver had said Southampton was full of tourists during the summer. All the same, it wouldn't do to let Nigel hear her American accent again. Fortunately, he was still sitting at the bar and showed no inclination to move. Tracey smiled at her companion after clearing her throat. "I'm on what you'd call a working holiday. Touring your cathedrals," she added, hoping that sounded plausible.

"Lovely. And have you been to Winchester?"

"No. I've just arrived." Tracey's glance dropped as she considered what to say next. Her fingers looked pale against the glass of warm red-brown wine. Fortunately no one knew what a nervous stranglehold she had on the stemware. If only she could have relaxed like Ferdie, who sighed again just then, disdaining the smoky room, the worn vinyl furniture, and the noisy voices of the buffet patrons. Tracey was wondering how to corral something to eat for herself when she realized that she'd ignored some conversation.

". . . actually one of the finest on the south coast. At least that's my opinion," the woman at her elbow was saying. "You shouldn't miss it, at any rate." She paused, looking to Tracey for affirmation.

The other's thoughts raced frantically. *What* wasn't she supposed to miss, for Lord's sake? "I certainly don't intend to," she said faintly.

"Fortunately, there's excellent local transportation. No need to take a tour." The woman looked severely at her over the top of her glass. "Just go down to the station in the center of town. There's a splendid bus schedule—one every hour."

"That certainly is convenient," Tracey floundered, and put down her sherry, wishing she hadn't ordered it. Alcohol on an empty stomach wasn't helping.

"Just ask the driver, if the bus isn't marked Winchester," Ferdie's owner went on.

Tracey sighed with relief. Of course! The cathedral. "Actually, I hope to go on Sunday," she explained, happy that she could tell the truth for a change. "It would be nice to hear the choir or attend a service."

"A capital idea! You should enjoy it tremendously." The woman put down her empty glass with visible regret and made motions of leaving. "Now, where did I put Ferdie's leash? It's a pity I have to leave you, my dear. I've enjoyed our little chat so much. Oh, aren't you going to eat a bite of lunch?" The last came as Tracey retrieved her purse and stood up beside her.

"Not now." Tracey was determined to use Ferdie and his owner as safe convoy from the room, since

Nigel was still sitting at the bar. "Actually, I may have something sent up to my room. It seems easier."

"I know what you mean, dear. A pretty girl sitting alone . . ." She cast a disapproving glance at the men around them after she'd secured Ferdie's leash and persuaded him to get to his feet. "Who knows what would happen?"

Tracey could have told her that she needn't worry, that normally the patrons would have held no problems for her at all. Instead she concentrated on ignoring the tempting smells of the buffet as they passed the table. For an instant she considered filching a sausage roll and leaving some money beside the platter, but another look at the individuals still waiting their turn in line made her discard the idea. She could only hope that the Poseidon had such a thing as room service in the middle of the day.

She parted from Ferdie and his owner on cordial terms with a heartfelt invitation from the older woman to join them the next day for "a bit of sherry," if convenient. Ferdie seconded the invitation with a slow wagging of his tail. At least, that's what his owner claimed he was doing. Tracey suspected it was because he'd caught a whiff of fresh air coming in from the lobby door.

When he and his mistress had left the hotel, Tracey didn't waste any time stepping in the elevator and pushing the button for her floor. There still wasn't any sign of Nigel on her trail, and she leaned against the side of the elevator after the doors closed to let out a sigh of relief. His presence on the hotel scene had been a setback she hadn't expected. Now she was going to have to look around corners every time she left her room.

When she got out of the elevator at her floor, she hurried down the carpeted hallway past two inadequate fire doors which led to the older section of the building, where her room was located. She had her key in hand by the time she reached her door, and it was the matter of a moment to unlock it and hastily shove it open.

She stepped inside, and still without a wasted motion turned to close it firmly behind her—at the last moment even sliding on the chain lock.

"Very commendable," said a deep masculine voice close by, "but a little late. Wait a minute—don't faint, you little idiot! My God! You'd have broken your neck if I hadn't caught you."

"You!" There was dazed disbelief in the word. Tracey raised her head from Bart Jennings' shirtfront where he'd clutched her to him. "You scared me out of fifteen years' growth." She drew a startled breath. "Now what are you doing?"

"Scalping you in the bargain." He was pulling off the blond wig as he spoke. "It's not hard to figure out unless you've had a liquid lunch. And you must have had, because you smell like a distillery." He draped her none too gently on the narrow single bed and turned to plug in the electric kettle. "You'd better sober up, and fast."

"If you plan to do it with coffee, I'll pour it down the drain. . . ."

"What do you have against coffee?"

"Not a damned thing," she snarled, temper replacing the fright which had made her pulse race like a derby contender. "Only I haven't had anything except coffee and a package of cookies since I left London at dawn."

"There must have been something else."

"One small glass of sherry." She put her hands up to her temples then and pressed hard. "Why in the deuce am I explaining things to you?"

"Because if you don't, the maid'll find you in little pieces when she changes the towels. That's what you deserve after doing your disappearing act this morning."

"Oh, that." Tracey hedged as she saw him position the only upholstered chair in the room and sit down on it. "It might take quite a while to explain the whole thing."

"I don't doubt it, so you might as well make up your mind to tell the truth the first time. Otherwise—" He let the word hang ominously.

"Otherwise what?"

He leaned back and surveyed her sardonically. "Otherwise I'll have to find a way to persuade you. And I can guarantee that you won't like my methods."

Her eyebrows went up. "That doesn't surprise me."

"Sarcasm won't help," he went on relentlessly. His glance raked her slumped figure on the edge of the bed, as if he'd just become conscious of how pale her cheeks were against her fiery tousled hair. "You look grim. What in the devil have you been doing since you left London?"

She struggled to her feet then and went over to the dressing table. "Supporting British Rail most of the time. Lord, it feels good to get rid of that wig," she added, brushing her hair vigorously. She put the brush down on the glass-topped surface and met his glance in the mirror with a crooked smile. "At least let me order something from room service. I must be entitled to a last meal before you pronounce sentence. Didn't the Magna Carta decree it?"

"Remind me to give you a history book for Christmas." He got up to unplug the kettle when it started to steam and poured boiling water over instant coffee in a cup. Tracey thought he was going to offer it to her and was all set to refuse when he calmly took a swallow and carried the cup back to his chair. "My breakfast was a little thin, too. This will give me strength to go out and bring you a doggie bag." When she started to frown, he explained. "There's no room service in this hotel except breakfast. I had plenty of time to read the rules on the back of your door while I was cooling my heels."

Her frown deepened. "That's another thing—how did you get in here in the first place?"

"I bribed the hall porter—told him you were my fiancée and I wanted to surprise you. He did everything but roll out the red carpet. You must have overtipped him when you checked in." Bart took another swallow of coffee. "Maybe he could sneak some food up, though."

He looked toward the telephone, but Tracey nipped that in the bud. "No way. There's a central switchboard and the woman in charge acts like the matron in an Albanian road gang. If she thought I had a man in this room, I'd be put in the stocks on the town Common."

He shook his head as if to clear it. "No doubt about it—I'll have to buy you a history book."

"Well, maybe I'm exaggerating a little, but you should see her. She didn't even approve of Ian."

"I'll take your word for it," he started to say, and then snarled, "Who the hell is Ian?"

Tracey leaned across and carefully straightened

the electric kettle on its asbestos pad as she stalled for time. If she told Bart all about her plans for a job interview at Ardsley later in the afternoon, he wasn't above locking her in the room and taking the key. It would be better to offer an edited version after it was safely over.

"Just a taxi driver who brought me here from the train station," she said finally. "I thought we were talking about food. How did we get sidetracked?"

Bart got reluctantly to his feet and replaced his coffeecup on the tray. "All right. I'll go out and find some. If I use the back fire stairs, nobody should be any wiser."

"I hope it doesn't take you long."

"It just depends on how far I have to go," he said frankly. "I don't feel a damned bit sorry for you. If you'd followed orders in the first place, you'd be having a late lunch in London now and Stella wouldn't be . . ." He broke off, as if he'd said more than he planned.

Tracey's eyes narrowed. "What about Stella?"

"I'll tell you when I come back. Is there any food served in the bar downstairs?"

"Yes, but be careful if you go in there. My old chum Nigel from Kensington High Street was sitting at the bar when I left a little while ago. I was terrified that he'd recognize me."

"Why didn't you tell me earlier?"

"Because you shoved everything else from my mind." She rubbed the back of her neck fretfully. "Popping up here like a genie from a bottle."

He came over then and pulled her hand away, substituting his own fingers to massage the tight muscles at her nape. "Genies don't pop—they ooze.

At least, that's what I've been told. Relax, or this won't do a bit of good."

Tracey tried to do as he asked, but it was almost impossible when he stood so close. She was tantalizingly aware of his virile strength as those lean fingers stroked the back of her neck. If she let her head fall forward onto his shoulder, she'd have to combat the faint tempting fragrance of his after-shave or the mingled masculine trademarks of clean starched linen and tweed. Not only that, probably Stella Frome had rested against the shoulder of that same sport coat not long before.

"Relax," Bart said again, giving her an admonitory shake. "Maybe this therapy would work better if you went over and sat on the bed." He shoved her in that direction, but when she perched rigidly on the edge of it, he gave her an irritated, almost baffled glance. "Forget it—the mattress is too low." He gestured toward the bathroom. "A hot tub might help. You can try it while I go out and get something for us to eat."

His departure was so abrupt that Tracey was still staring after him wide-eyed and breathless when the hall door closed behind him.

7

A half-hour later, when he returned, Tracey had managed to pull herself together. She'd changed into a fresh blouse and skirt, hanging her navy-blue blazer on the back of a straight chair so she'd be ready for her trip later to Ardsley.

Bart favored her with an appraising glance as she shut the door behind him. "You look better. Where do you want this stuff?" He indicated the jumble of plastic bags he was clutching. "Get the milk, will you? It's slipping."

Tracey hastily extricated a waxed container of milk and deposited it on the windowsill at the end of the room. "That dressing table over there will have to do for the rest. If I'd known I'd be entertaining, I'd have asked for a suite."

"Well, don't get upset about it. Remember, if I leave, I take the sandwiches with me." He looked around. "There's just one cup. Is there a glass in the bathroom?"

"Two of them. I raided the maid's cart while you were gone."

"Good enough." He stripped off his coat and then stood looking for a place to put it.

"Drape it over my blazer. There were only three hangers in the closet to start with. Ummm, ham sandwiches," she said, undoing the paper wrappings. "They look wonderful. How far did you have to go to get them?"

"A few blocks. The food service downstairs was finished. Incidentally, there wasn't anybody with a mustache sitting at the bar."

"That's a relief. I must have fooled Nigel, after all. It's a good thing I was wearing the wig," she added as she brought the bathroom glasses and poured the milk. "We have one chair and one bed. Take your choice."

"This is handy." He sat on the edge of the bed after putting his glass of milk on the table near the headboard. "I think they stuffed the mattress with cobblestones they had left over from the city streets." He shoved her pillow aside, trying to get in a comfortable position against the headboard. "I told you that you should have stayed in London."

"That remark sounds vaguely familiar." Tracey kept her attention on the napkin in her lap.

"I thought I was being uncommonly tactful," he said over a bite of sandwich. "Why did you rush off like that? Afraid for your virtue? I told you that you didn't have to worry."

Tracey tried to hide her indignation, but she was only partially successful. "I explained the reason in my note. My sex life—or lack of it," she added sweetly, "had nothing whatsoever to do with my decision."

Bart had put his glasses on to investigate the rest of his sandwich, and he peered over them to survey her owlishly. "I'm not so sure. You were damned curious about Stella."

"Naturally. Any woman would be, since you keep dragging her into the conversation. I gather that she wasn't thrilled when you detoured to Southampton."

"Now, that's where you're wrong." The spectacles were shoved up again and he reached for his milk. "She was the one who drove me down."

Tracey almost choked on a bit of sandwich. "Good Lord! You mean she's here now?"

"In the general neighborhood. I don't know why you're so surprised. I told you last night she knew Oliver, so she could help me wangle an invitation to Ardsley."

"You mean . . . ?"

"Just that. She did, I did, and he did. Stella decided to join the party because she didn't have anything special planned in town."

"I'll bet!"

"Considering your limited acquaintance, you seem to harbor an unwarranted prejudice." He took another bite of sandwich and chewed it reflectively. "That's a diplomatic way of saying you sound jealous as hell."

"Jealousy has nothing to do with it," Tracey shot back. "I just don't see why the two of you had to follow me down here and confuse things. Probably this is all fun and games."

"Oh, sure. I was doubled over with laughter when I saw you playing chicken with that bus on Kensington High Street yesterday," he drawled.

"I've already thanked you for rescuing me—"

"Good God! Do you think I'm hanging around just to squeeze more gratitude out of you?" He discarded the remainder of his sandwich as if he'd suddenly lost his appetite and stood up to plug in the kettle. "There's no use discussing it any longer. Just stay out of the way while you're in the neighborhood—that's all I ask."

"Well, thanks very much."

He totally ignored her sarcasm, using the time while waiting for the boiling water to discard his lunch remnants in the wastebasket and rinse out the milk glass. The silence lengthened between them until he'd made a cup of tea, using one of the bags that the hotel furnished on the tray. After that, he said stiffly, "I *would* like to hear what you have scheduled for the rest of the day."

"So you can give it your okay?" she asked flippantly. It was hard to act as if his disapproval didn't bother her, when it did. But there was no way she could apologize without admitting that sheer bloody-minded jealousy was the reason she'd lost her temper in the first place.

Bart didn't rise to her taunt either; he merely waited in the middle of the room and sipped his tea.

The brooding treatment worked, as he undoubtedly knew it would. Tracey finally capitulated. "The taxi driver's coming back at three to take me around."

"Around where?"

"The local places of interest." She was prepared then, because she'd known this would be in store. Bart wasn't the type to forget any pertinent details, no matter how many red herrings she dragged in. "I've always wanted to see the New Forest, and he's sure to know some more places of interest, as well."

Bart leaned against the corner of the dressing table, completely at ease. "I wouldn't be surprised if he took you to Milton Abbas for the rest of the afternoon."

Her forehead creased. "Milton Abbas? What's that?"

"Milton Abbey and St. Catherine's Chapel. They tell me it's a favorite of women visitors."

Tracey shrugged helplessly. "I must have read the wrong tourist guidebooks. They mentioned the cathedrals at Salisbury and Winchester, but not Milton Abbey. What's so great about that chapel?"

"St. Catherine was the patron saint of spinsters. I just thought you might like to pay your respects."

"I should have known. What am I supposed to do when I get there, so that St. Catherine can work her miracle?"

Bart kept his voice solemn as his expression. "You say something like 'St. Catherine, St. Catherine, lend me thine aid. And grant that I *never* may die an old maid.' "

Tracey drew in a strangled breath. "Unfortunately I don't think I can work in St. Catherine this afternoon. I'll have to settle for visiting the manor at Beaulieu or ask Ian to drive me to Winchester."

"You'd better save the cathedral for tomorrow," Bart ordered, reverting to his normal crisp tones. "The New Forest and all the stuff at Beaulieu will fill your afternoon. Beaulieu's more than just a country estate—their motor museum is probably the best in England." He frowned as if a thought had just occurred to him. "I didn't know you were interested in vintage cars."

"I'm not, especially. It's Beaulieu's Abbey and the Palace House I want to see."

"But they've been thoroughly publicized already. I shouldn't think you'd find anything new for research there." He stared at her suspiciously. "Exactly what did you have in mind?"

The last of Tracey's sandwich slipped from her nervous fingers. By the time she'd scrabbled on the worn linoleum to retrieve the piece of crust, she'd thought of an answer. "The weekly medieval banquets they hold in the thirteenth-century banqueting hall. Ian knows some of the local people who are involved, and I could get some human-interest items that Oscar might like."

Bart took a final sip of tea and walked into the bathroom to rinse out the cup. "Want me to fix you some tea?" he asked when he came back into the bedroom again.

"No, thanks. Not right now."

He nodded and put the cup back down on the tray. "You've heard, of course, that they're doing medieval banquets at Ardsley House, too."

"Ian did mention something about it." She shot him a defiant glance. "Actually, I thought I might take a quick look at the banqueting hall there, too— so I could compare the two places."

Bart scraped his thumb along his jaw as if considering possibilities. "The driver—this Ian you're talking about—he'll be with you?"

Tracey could see him weakening and said quickly, "Yes, of course."

"And you'll wear the wig?" He gestured toward the blond hairpiece she'd left on the dressing table.

She raised her palm solemnly. "Every minute. Seeing Nigel downstairs convinced me. I may even sleep in the darned thing."

"All right. But I'm only giving in because you'd probably pull some other caper if I tried to lean on you. Remember, though, any funny stuff and I'll call Oscar. You'll be on a plane at Heathrow before you know what's happening. Is that clear?"

"It's because of men like you that the women's rights movement ever got started in the first place."

"Did you hear what I said?"

"Of course I heard what you said. Obviously you didn't hear what *I* said," she retorted in some annoyance.

"We'll go over it another time. Right now I have to meet Stella and drive back to Ardsley. I'll try to call tonight, but if I can't I'll check with you tomorrow morning at the latest. Do you understand?"

"The mind boggles—but I'll struggle and do my best. Give my best to Miss Frome." He had the door halfway open before she remembered one more thing. "I forgot to pay you for lunch. Just a minute until I get my purse—"

The slam of the door behind him cut her off in mid-sentence, and Tracey nodded, thoroughly pleased. She'd had a feeling that he wouldn't like her mentioning money or paying him back. Deliberately she took her memo book from her purse and made a note to add lunch money to what she already owed him for one night's lodging in London.

She also made a mental note to make sure there were no onlookers when Ian deposited her at the service entrance of Ardsley House that afternoon.

When his taxi arrived at the Poseidon a little later, he got out quickly to open the door for her. "Right on time—just as I promised," he said, greeting her. "Mind your head now when you get in."

Tracey waited until they were on their way out of the hotel's curving drive before she asked, "We're going to Ardsley House first, aren't we? I'd hate to be late for that job interview with your aunt."

"That's right." He turned into a one-way street on the other side of the Common, which led back toward the center of town. "You'll get to see part of the New Forest on the way, so it's not a total loss for you. Maybe another day I can drive you to Milton Abbas—"

Tracey cut him off before he could even get started on that tack. "I doubt if I'll have time while I'm here." If she hadn't known better, she would have suspected that Bart had put him up to it. Either that, or the British male ego was programmed to believe that every woman who came to the south of England needed St. Catherine's help.

Ian didn't waste any time cutting through the busy streets of Southampton as he angled for an express highway which paralleled the dock area and passed the tall chimneys and industrial plants of the busy port.

Once they'd gotten beyond the western edge of Southampton Water, the countryside softened and mellowed. The almost solid phalanx of suburban apartment buildings became thready and then changed to scattered homes whose flower gardens were just coming to life after a late spring. The busy expressway narrowed and then disappeared completely, turning into a pleasant winding country road.

As if in honor of the transformation, the sun came out and the damp paving stones steamed under its late-afternoon rays.

Then suddenly they were in a woodland with oaks and beeches so thick that Tracey almost expected Robin Hood and his band to appear as they wound through the quiet glades.

"I thought you'd like it." Ian's glance met her entranced one in the rearview mirror. He was smiling with pride as he gestured at the trees on either side of the road. "Five thousand acres of forest, and it's almost the same as it was when it belonged to William the Conqueror. Only in those days the New Forest was strictly for royal hunting. Now we have over a hundred square miles in public ownership."

"I had no idea," Tracey said truthfully. "You wouldn't think there was anything around for miles."

"Don't you believe it! This part of the forest is full of animals. 'Course, the king's wild boar and wolf are gone, but there are plenty of deer left. You won't see much of them in the day—they come out to graze on the heath at night."

"Is Ardsley House here in the Forest?"

"Of course. But all the estates and homes have to conform to zoning rules. Cattle and deer—even the forest ponies—are allowed to wander along the lanes here. The laws go back to the Saxon days. One of them decrees that animals have the right-of-way over all traffic."

"I promise not to argue with a pony or a deer at an intersection," Tracey assured him. "What happens if they want to eat your vegetable garden?"

"You don't have to sit still for that. There's a nice fence around most of Ardsley's grounds just to take care of things like that. The estate's only a little farther along the way here." Ian took his eyes off the road long enough to glance at his watch. "Too bad there isn't more time. Otherwise I could take you to see Sir Arthur Conan Doyle's grave at Minstead churchyard and the place where they built the ships for Trafalgar at Bucklers Hard."

"They sound fascinating, but I'd really like to know more about Ardsley House before we arrive. Has Mr. Rustad's family owned it for long?"

"I'd say about three generations. That doesn't mean much, since the place was built around 1750 or so. Aunt Phoebe says the last death duties put Oliver Rustad in a worse hole than ever and that he'll be lucky to work out of it to save his inheritance. He's hoping the tours and banquet scheme will succeed, or he'll have to sell the place."

Ian braked and turned the taxi into a narrow lane leading upward through a grove of trees. The car passed over a cattle grid as they left the highway, and then Tracey concentrated on trying to see past some leafy branches for a first glimpse of the estate.

When they came upon it a minute or two later, she was pleasantly surprised. Ian's talk of straitened finances hadn't prepared her for the expanse of velvety green lawn edging the smooth curved drive or the three-story fieldstone manor house which looked big enough to house a regiment. Besides the manor with its turrets and mullioned windows, there seemed to be a great number of outbuildings for staff, stables, and garages.

"If Mr. Rustad's feeling the pinch, he does it in style," she commented wryly as Ian braked at a door some distance from the main entrance to the estate.

"I didn't mean that he was down to his last Constable or Van Dyke," Ian said, turning off the engine and grinning over his shoulder. "The Rustads lived in the city before Oliver inherited this estate. If things get threadbare here, he can go back to his flat in Mayfair. And Aunt Phoebe says he owns some mews cottages for extra income."

"Is he married?"

"Not that I've heard. The latest rumor is that he's courting a woman with plenty of brass."

Tracey stepped out when he opened the taxi door.

"Well, I'd better see if I can get this job and add a little brass to my own bank account. Do I just knock on the nearest door?"

"No. Come along—I'll take you to my aunt. The live-in staff quarters are in this wing for the most part." He led the way past a raised bed of tulips where the bulbs were just starting to grow. On closer inspection, Tracey saw there was a generous helping of weeds to compete with the flowers. Ian followed her glance before he opened the door, saying, "They're short of outside staff, too. Do you have a green thumb?"

"Not really. I struggle with crocuses in a window box."

"Then you'd better stick to dining-room help. Mind the step there, and straight ahead through the hallway. If Auntie's not in her rooms here, she's probably down in the kitchen." He led the way through a narrow, dimly-lit corridor, finally stopping to knock on a door with a brass nameplate.

Tracey was still trying to decipher the dim engraving on the metal when the door opened and she saw a short, pudding-dumpling figure of a woman in a neat gray dress.

Ian leaned over to kiss the middle-aged woman's cheek before she had a chance to speak. "Aunt Phoebe, love. Here's your newest. Tracey, this is my aunt, Mrs. Jenks." He waved her on into the housekeeper's sitting room. "I'll leave you two and go wait in the car."

"That's a good lad," his aunt said, just before a buzzer sounded on the old-fashioned call board hanging near the door. "Wouldn't you know! Just when I try to get a free minute," she said with an apologetic grimace at her callers. "Sit down, both of you, while I answer this."

Tracey perched on the edge of a straight chair and Ian went over to sit on a mauve upholstered sofa that looked like a prop from a Valentino movie. A crocheted afghan made up of multicolored squares was thrown over the velour back. Tracey noticed that the same type of squares were under the vase on a drop-leaf table and the bronze head of Lord Nelson which sat atop a small television set. Even the tea cozy on a tray by the window was made with the same crochet stitch. Her survey was interrupted at that point by Mrs. Jenks slamming down the receiver.

"That girl hasn't the sense she was born with. Everything's a shocking muddle." The housekeeper came back to the middle of the room and eyed Tracey hopefully. "Do you cook?"

"Just omelets and casseroles for the most part," Tracey said truthfully.

The housekeeper sighed and then nodded. "Well, I'm sure you'll do fine as a waitress tomorrow night. I'm sorry not to have longer to talk to you, but Mr. Oliver's brought house guests with him. Cook is at the dentist and the girl who's helping out doesn't know a Yorkshire pudding from a trifle. Probably they'll both taste the same at dinner if I don't go down and straighten her out." She walked over to open the door. "Now, then—Tracey, is it? Report here tomorrow at four. We serve the banquet at seven but there's a fair lot of preparation first in the dining hall. You should be finished by ten, and we always furnish transportation back to Southampton for our temporary help. You'll have time for tea before the banquet. Is there anything else?"

Tracey bit her lip, trying to think. "Clothes. What should I wear?"

"We supply an Elizabethan serving costume and a mobcap that covers your hair." She eyed the other's blond curls and went on to say, "Just as well in your case. Some of the visitors are a bit . . . boisterous."

"She means they get snockered on the ale," Ian put in, earning a glare from his aunt.

"Most of them are very well-behaved." The housekeeper looked at the watch she had pinned on her ample bust. "I must get along now. Mr. Oliver doesn't like it if dinner isn't just right. He's brought Miss Frome and some important visitor from overseas."

"We won't keep you, love," Ian told her, leading Tracey out into the hallway. "Everything will turn out grand."

His aunt snorted. "Much you know about it."

Tracey cut in hastily, "Thank you very much, Mrs. Jenks. I'll be here tomorrow. Right on time, I promise."

Ian waited until the two of them were back beside the taxi before he solemnly shook her hand. "Welcome to the ranks of the laboring class."

Tracey grinned in response, scarcely able to believe her good fortune. She had a perfect excuse for peering in the corners of Ardsley now. All she had to do was come early for work the next day and leave late. She was about to get in the car, when a look around at the deserted drive made her decide not to postpone all her exploring until then. As long as she stayed near the outbuildings and the staff quarters, she had every chance of avoiding the owner of Ardsley or his house guests.

"I'd like to stay a little longer now," she told Ian.

"Your aunt wouldn't mind if we explored, would she?"

His hand remained on the car-door handle as he frowned slightly. "I don't suppose she'd object. Mind you, the main rooms of the place won't be open for visitors now. The toffs don't want to be disturbed when there are no tours scheduled." He paused. "There's still time for a cuppa at Beaulieu if we hurry, and the Palace House there puts this one to shame."

"I'm not terribly keen on stately homes. It's the grounds that fascinate me," she said, improvising hastily. "I spent an entire day wandering around Hampton Court admiring the plantings. Is there anything special here?"

"Just a long reflecting pool on the other side of the main wing, but the private rooms overlook it, and I don't think we should wander around there now."

"Of course not, but what about the outbuildings?" she said, waving a casual hand toward the ones just beyond the staff quarters. "It won't hurt to walk that way, will it?"

Ian stared at her, plainly perplexed, and then gave in. "If that's what turns you on. I didn't know tourists ever wanted to stare at a bunch of dustbins, though." He gestured toward a line of garbage cans as they went around a corner.

It was difficult to refute such unassailable logic, and Tracey walked on, trying to appear fascinated by the utility area of the hall. It was a little easier when they came to the garages, where a vintage Rolls and a Mini—along with a scarlet sports car— were lodged. "I suppose the Rolls belongs to Mr. Rustad."

"Well, it's not Aunt Phoebe's." Ian was clearly regretting his overlooked teatime. "See any other place you fancy?" he said when Tracey hesitated at a fork in the path beyond the corner of the garage.

"It does look a little shabby here," she admitted after looking at two derelict storage buildings halfway down the slope, where the estate grounds turned to rough pasture. She let her glance wander back to the garage again and then frowned as she noticed the second story of the building. "Who lives up there? The chauffeur?"

"Not likely—this isn't Buckingham," Ian said cynically. "They're just storage rooms now. Mr. Rustad doesn't come down often, and it costs too much to have a lot of staff sitting around. He *does* have a man of affairs who keeps things in order here most of the time. An ambitious bloke."

"Oh?" Tracey tried to sound casual. "What's his name?"

"Nigel something-or-other—you can find out tomorrow. Aunt Phoebe says he's a wonder at refurbishing things, and some of that stuff has been around so long it takes a lot of fixing."

Tracey felt a surge of excitement. He must be talking about Nigel Pelham, of course! How convenient for the man to be manager of a place like Ardsley. It made his extracurricular activities so simple.

"You'll have to ask Auntie about it tomorrow," Ian said, cagily edging her back toward the car as they talked. "I know the stuff they're working on is stored in the same wing as her apartment. The furniture's too valuable to leave untended, and the insurance chaps have to make sure nothing's missing. You wait here . . ." He veered off the path and dodged behind a mammoth rhododendron bush which was planted by the door of the staff quarters they'd gone through earlier. He beckoned then to Tracey who had hesitated before following him through the shrubbery. "Take a gander through this window. It's bloody dark," he complained an instant later as she came and looked over his shoulder. "All you can see are a couple of pieces, and they're pretty dim."

Tracey forgot about the damp earth and weeds of the shrubbery bed when she brushed aside a cobweb and pressed her nose against the glass, trying to hide her excitement as she peered eagerly into the storeroom.

Ian was right in his appraisal—it *was* a gloomy old place. Then she found herself staring at the outlines of the piece closest to the window, and every other thought promptly left her mind. It was the same Regency worktable that had been displayed in the Kensington High Street arcade just the day before. She knew it! Despite the pile of newspapers haphazardly atop it and the varnish cans scattered on the floor around its base, it was impossible to cloak the fine lines of the old piece. "Well, I'll be . . ." she murmured incredulously.

"See something you like?" Ian had pulled back and was wiping his hands on his worn tweed pants. "Hullo—that sounds like company." He put up a restraining hand, motioning Tracey to stay where she was next to the window. Standing immobile, they caught just a glimpse of a masculine figure going down the path to their left and then striding across the forecourt toward the garage.

"It's all right—I recognized the bloke," Ian said. "It's a gardener who doubles as Mr. Rustad's chauffeur. Looks like he's going down to get one of the cars."

"Let's get out of here. I don't want to be discovered hanging around if someone's leaving," Tracey told him.

Ian didn't waste any time following her to the taxi; clearly he wasn't keen to be caught trespassing when Oliver Rustad emerged from the front door.

Ian turned his car toward the road again but followed a lower drive than the one they'd used coming in. They had safely turned onto the winding pavement which would lead them back to the edge of the New Forest before Ian, who had been checking his rearview mirror, announced that the vintage Rolls from Ardsley was coming up fast behind them. "They must be driving to Southampton. Can't see who's in the back until they overtake us."

Tracey had been sitting well back in the corner of the taxi's rear seat. When she heard his comment, she deliberately dropped her purse onto the bottom of the car and reached down to pick it up—managing to stay out of sight until the limousine was safely past.

"Seemed to be three of them," Ian announced when she surfaced again. "There was a beautiful blond bird with Mr. Rustad."

"Miss Frome."

"You know her?" Ian sounded surprised and impressed.

"A distant acquaintance," Tracey said, happy that the distance was getting greater by the minute. "Is it too late for that cup of tea you mentioned? Maybe we could go someplace nearby."

"Right you are! Beaulieu isn't far from here, and there's a place that serves teas there."

"That sounds fine." Just so long as it was away from that Rolls and its occupants, Tracey thought dismally. It was ridiculous for her to feel discouraged suddenly just because Bart was probably going to spend the rest of the day with another woman. After all, she hardly knew the man. Not only that, she'd quarreled with him most of the time they'd been together. She thought about that discouraging fact as Ian drove along the road which twisted through the picturesque countryside.

"Nice, eh?" He gestured as they went past an old inn whose sign proclaimed that it had been there since the fifteenth-century.

"Lovely." Traced tried to sound enthusiastic. "Is it much farther to where we're going?"

"About five minutes or so to the village of Beaulieu, where you can see the estate. We'll stop in the car park and walk across to the tearoom. It's not far to the Motor Museum, if you want to go there later." When she didn't respond to his last suggestion, the taxi driver shot her a quick look over his shoulder. "If you feel like it, of course. It would be a shame to miss it, though. They even have Sir Malcolm Campbell's race car there—the one that broke all the speed records."

"Let's see how much time there is after we eat. Actually, I get paid for reporting on Hepplewhite and Chippendale—not vintage race cars."

Ian's shrug was eloquent, showing that for his money there was no comparison.

They weren't the only people who chose to visit Beaulieu that afternoon. The car park for the famous country estate was more than half full. After Ian locked the taxi, he led her through groups of tourists strolling on the hard-surfaced paths. "The wind's picking up, but at least it isn't raining," he commented, buttoning his short, thick jacket. "Mind you, some hot tea won't go amiss. I was sure we'd get some from Aunt Phoebe, but she didn't even have the kettle on."

Tracey tried to keep from smiling. She'd heard about Australians stopping the world while they boiled the billy at four o'clock. Ian's remark proved that the British apparently felt the same way.

"The gift shop's there on the right," he was going on, "and they serve teas at that cafeteria just beyond. Nothing fancy, but we can sit by the window and get a view of the Palace House and the museum."

"This place is huge—it would make three or four of Ardsley House." Tracey stepped aside so that a couple with a pram could get past them on the narrow path. "It must take a mint to keep these estates functioning."

"Plenty of brass, that's certain. That's why Mr. Rustad's having problems." Ian, who had been strolling beside her with his hands in his pockets, stopped suddenly. "Speak of the devil—there he is. I thought they were on the way to Southampton."

Tracey drew a stricken breath as she caught a glimpse of the trio walking briskly toward them. Even though they were still a half-block away, she recognized Stella Frome, in a coat of royal blue which contrasted elegantly with her pale blond hair. The man beside her was tall and fair, too, and must have been Oliver Rustad. There wasn't much doubt about it, because she could easily identify the man on the other side of Stella. This time, he wasn't leaning against a bar or displaying antique furniture, but there was no disguising Nigel Pelham's almost saturnine dark looks.

"Oh, Lord!" Tracey groaned. There wasn't any way to escape meeting the trio face to face on the path unless she bolted abruptly back to the taxi—a move sure to arouse their undivided attention. All she could do was keep going with her head down and pray that no one would pay any attention to them.

Unfortunately she'd forgotten about Ian.

Either he was intent on showing his familiarity with the local gentry or simply exuding a sense of neighborliness, because he boomed out, "Afternoon, Mr. Rustad," when they drew abreast of the trio. "Nice to see you down this way. You, too, Nigel."

Oliver Rustad hesitated, looking flustered for a minute. "Ah, yes—Ian, isn't it?" His glance went to Tracey, but when she stared pointedly into the distance, he nodded pleasantly again to the younger man. "Enjoy yourself."

Ian had to quicken his steps to catch up with Tracey. "I thought you'd like to speak to them—being so interested in Ardsley and all," he said. "You could have told him you were going to work at the banquet tomorrow. It never hurts to have a friend in court, you know."

"Never mind that. Just look back over your shoulder—casually," she warned before he could follow her direction. "As if you were admiring the scenery or something. Find out if they're staring after us."

His mouth dropped open, and then he closed it again before he did as she asked. "Blimey! How did you know? They've just started on." He snapped his fingers. "That's right! You said you knew the lady. S'funny she didn't say anything."

"They're going on to the car park?"

"That's right." He risked another glance over his

shoulder and nodded emphatically. Then he became aware of Tracey's pale face. "You sure you feel all right?"

She nodded, oblivious of his concern. Just then she was still shaking after receiving Nigel Pelham's narrowed glance, suspecting that her blond wig hadn't proved any disguise at all. The fact that the trio had lingered on the path showed that some kind of discussion had taken place after the meeting.

If only Bart were around so she could ask him what to do next. She would have given a very great deal to have one of his broad shoulders to lean on just then.

Her unhappiness must have been evident, because Ian cleared his throat and put a hand under her elbow. "You'll be better after a nice cuppa," he promised. "That's all you need to put you on top of the heap again."

He was trying to be tactful, and Tracey appreciated his efforts. It was just a pity that, in this case, he simply didn't know what he was talking about.

8

When he drove her back to Southampton a little later, she chose to be deliberately vague about her future plans. She thanked him for taking her to Ardsley and gave him a sizable tip over his quoted price, carefully explaining that she didn't know her itinerary for the following day. "I'll probably take a bus to Winchester in the morning or something like that," she stalled.

"Shall I drive you out to Ardsley House in the afternoon? I could do it on the cheap, since there's no sightseeing."

"I'll have to wait and see. Give me the number of your company and then if I call, I'll be sure to ask for you."

"Righto." He fished a creased card from the glove compartment and handed it to her. "Best service in town."

"I know, and I'll probably see you again before I leave Southampton. Oh, one more thing . . ."

Ian was turning the key in the ignition but he stopped and looked inquiringly at her through the open car window. "Forget something?"

She shook her head. "I'd just appreciate it if you

didn't volunteer any information about what we did this afternoon—if you happen to see Nigel or Mr. Rustad again soon."

"Was that why you were looking so upset? It was Nigel, wasn't it?" Ian's jaw took on a pugnacious angle. "Somebody should have warned you about him. He has a rotten reputation with the local women. I'd give him a wide berth when you go out to work at the House tomorrow. He might be around scouting for new talent," Ian went on. "If he gives you any trouble, tip off Aunt Phoebe. She claims he's a good manager but she won't stand for any hanky-panky with her help. Everybody toes the mark in her domain—even Mr. Rustad. Although he's not the type to pick up local birds. Especially—"

"—when he already has such a good-looking one staying for the weekend," Tracey finished for him. "Although I don't think that he's the man Miss Frome is after. Don't forget, there's an overseas celebrity staying at Ardsley, too."

"Well, it's a sure thing she wouldn't be wasting time with Nigel. His salary wouldn't keep her in shoes unless one of his flutters at the track paid off. Don't worry, Tracey." Ian bent to the ignition again. "I don't volunteer information about my fares. Doctors and priests aren't the only ones with privileged information. You'd be surprised what a taxi driver has to forget." He gave her a cheerful nod and drove off.

Tracey didn't waste any time going inside the hotel and taking the elevator to her room. Once there, she hastily packed her belongings and called the hall porter to carry them down to the lobby.

When she followed him downstairs, she was happy to see that a pleasant young woman had replaced the dragon who'd been on the reception desk when she checked in. "I'm awfully sorry but my plans have changed and I'm checking out," Tracey explained. "Naturally I'll pay for my room." She hauled out her traveler's checks and went on casually, "Oh, I'll need a taxi. Could you phone for one?" It seemed safe because the number for taxis posted above the switchboard didn't belong to Ian's company, and the reception clerk dialed it automatically.

When she completed the call, the woman came back to the counter and asked, "Do you have a forwarding address, Miss Winslow?"

"I'm a little up in the air about where I'm going to be." Tracey smiled disarmingly. "The tourist's lament, isn't it?"

The clerk gave a conventional answer although her expression revealed that she considered it a shocking waste of money to cross the Atlantic and pay for a hotel bed that wasn't going to be used.

The thrifty side of Tracey's nature agreed with her, but Nigel's almost sure recognition on the path at Beaulieu made her forget all about her budget. It wouldn't take long for him to link her with the Poseidon Hotel, which was why she had to make a hasty exit from the place.

"Are you expecting any calls, Miss Winslow?" the clerk asked, covering every eventuality. Probably because she dealt with harried tourists all the time.

"Not a one," Tracey replied, crossing her fingers behind her skirt. Bart would be on the phone without a doubt. Hopefully she could reach him before he discovered that she'd checked out.

When her taxi arrived a little later, Tracey inherited a taciturn driver who took her to the bus station without any questions or unnecessary conversation.

She hung around that unlovely ticket office long enough to garner some stares from locals who were waiting for their buses and a janitor who was mopping the linoleum. They probably thought it strange that five minutes later she flagged another taxi from the rank and drove off again.

This time the driver was more forthcoming. "Where can I drive you, lady? I have a nice little city tour that includes Arundel Tower and the Bargate. Then we drive to Catchcold Tower—"

Tracey's head came up. "What did you say? That last place?"

"Oh . . ." He looked amused. "Catchcold Tower. Are you interested?"

"I'll have to see it before I leave—that's for sure. Right now, though, I just want a bed-and-breakfast place. One that's clean and comfortable, please."

"Mrs. Lester runs nice accommodations. Not far from the Common. I've heard they're reasonable, too."

"Let's go and see."

A few minutes later he braked in front of a small and ancient brick house. A tidy sign in the front yard proclaimed "Bed and Breakfast—Reasonable Rates" and a minute or so later the landlady, who answered the taxi driver's knock, confirmed it.

She was thin and barely reached to his shoulder, but her sharp-eyed glance went quickly over Tracey and didn't miss a thing in its appraisal. "Come in, my dear. I'm Emma Lester. There's a nice single room at the front of the house if you'd like it. Let me show it to you."

The room was spartan in comforts but the linoleum was spotless and the dressing table was polished to such a gloss that it reflected the light from the dangling overhead fixture. The bed was made up with fresh, clean sheets, even though the mattress sagged, and Tracey nodded her acceptance without wasting any time. She could manage to walk around her open suitcases on the floor, and a bathroom down the hall didn't bother her. Especially since the alternative would have been listening for strange sounds at her door in the Poseidon.

When the taxi man had gone, Tracey convinced Mrs. Lester to "hot up" some soup for her and felt much better once she'd finished a bowl of it.

"One more thing," she asked the landlady. "Could I use your telephone, please? I'll be glad to pay charges."

Mrs. Lester gestured toward the front hall. "Just ask the operator for costs when you're finished. Sorry there isn't more privacy," she added when a couple came past them and walked up the stairs to their room.

"That's all right." Tracey thought it was probably just as well that there wasn't a secluded phone booth; she had no intention of holding a prolonged conversation with Bart or going into lengthy explanations about her move from the Poseidon. Any sensible man would be appreciative of such an action, telling her that she'd shown remarkably good sense and a splendid show of initiative.

She was thinking about that while she was waiting to get through to him at Ardsley—after being careful to say that his editor was calling.

When he came on the line, she found out immediately that he wasn't going to follow his prescribed role.

"What now?" were his brusque opening words.

She swallowed and then decided to follow her

script even though he wasn't cooperating. "Mr. Jennings? This is Tracey—Tracey Winslow."

"You don't have to spell it out. Once I spend the night with a woman, her name is indelibly engraved in my mind," he informed her. "That also entitles you to use my first name."

"But I didn't actually spend the night with you, and you know it. Not really . . ." Tracey suddenly became aware that the drape covering the archway to Mrs. Lester's living room was twitching, and she broke off. Damn it! she thought. Why hadn't she made her phone call *before* she'd left the hotel? Turning her back on the drape and the archway, she lowered her voice. "It doesn't matter. I just called to let you know that I've moved."

"You've what?"

"You heard me," she retorted more loudly, sounding just as cross as he did.

"Well, that's a damned silly thing to do. I know your room wasn't much, but all you had to do was change it for a better one. Unless"—there was a pause as another idea suddenly occurred to him— "unless you've had the good sense to go back to London as I told you. Is that what happened?"

"Certainly not. I'm still in Southampton."

"I might have known."

She didn't give him time to pursue that line of thought. "I just didn't want you to be surprised if you called the hotel tomorrow and found that I wasn't there."

"Thoughtful of you." His clipped comment showed that it wasn't anything of the kind. "If it wasn't the decor or the lack of amenities, what brought about the change?"

Tracey saw no point in being explicit. Especially

from the front hall of an English rooming house. "I met a man this afternoon—the one with the mustache—and I think he wanted to renew his acquaintance."

"Where in the hell were you?"

"Practically on your front doorstep. If you'd been with your friends, you'd have known."

"You mean he was along on that jaunt to . . ." Bart broke off, sounding as if he wasn't happy about the lack of privacy at his end, either. "Are you okay?"

"Fine," she said, glad finally to be open and above-board about something. "I just didn't want to cause complications."

"Something for which you've shown remarkable talent already."

Tracey decided to argue about that another time. "I'll do my best not to upset your weekend," she told him in tones guaranteed to raise his blood pressure. "I'll let you know later if I accomplish what I came for."

"You'll keep that elegant little nose of yours out of things, the way I told you," he retorted explosively. "Where the devil are you? I'll come and take you—"

Tracey gently replaced the telephone receiver on the hook in the middle of his last word. Afterward she rested her head against the cool plaster wall of Mrs. Lester's establishment, wondering if she'd done the right thing. It was all very well to sound as if she oozed confidence, but reality painted a grimmer picture. She'd have plenty of time to think about it when she was upstairs, incarcerated in a room scarcely larger than the swaybacked metal bed.

Her landlady popped her head around the living-room drape like a diminutive jack-in-the-box. "Everything all right, Miss Winslow?"

"Oh, yes," Tracey replied, straightening to smile at her. "Just gathering my strength before going to bed. It's been a long day."

Mrs. Lester chose to ignore the pleasantry. "It's nice that you know someone here in the neighborhood. Is he a gentleman friend?"

Tracey's smile faded. "Not really. A business associate, that's all."

"What a pity."

"Yes, I know. That's just what I was thinking. Good night, Mrs. Lester—I'll see you in the morning."

"Would you like me to waken you at any special time?"

"No, thanks." Tracey hesitated on the worn wooden stairs. "I brought an alarm clock. What time do you serve breakfast?"

"Eight o'clock to ten. The kettle's on before that if you'd like early tea."

"I'll wait and see." Tracey nodded and went up the stairs.

By morning, the weather at least had improved. There were blue skies with just a few lurking clouds and a sun that looked determined to stay around for a while.

Once Tracey had consumed Mrs. Lester's boiled egg with toast fingers and two cups of steaming coffee, she began to view the day with stirrings of anticipation.

Since she wasn't due at Ardsley House until late afternoon, it seemed sensible to remain out of contact until then. It was doubtful that Nigel Pelham would go beyond inquiring at the Poseidon, but she had no illusions about Bart on that score. He was just stubborn enough to ring up the local constabulary if he chose to locate her. And while the list of Southampton's bed-and-breakfast places was lengthy, it wasn't an impossible task.

Her landlady was running a dust cloth over a porcelain owl on the front-hall table when Tracey came down the stairs a half-hour later.

Mrs. Lester's glance went over the trim navy-blue blazer which Tracey was wearing with a gray-blue plaid skirt and a white cashmere pullover. "I always say that blonds should stick with blue. My daughter's hair used to be the same shade as yours. 'Course that's when she was just a girl—" she sighed reminiscently. "I hope you enjoy your day."

"Thank you. Oh, Mrs. Lester . . ." Tracey turned when she was halfway over the threshold as a sudden thought occurred to her. "I may be late getting in tonight. You don't lock the door or anything like that, do you?"

"I always do after eleven." The landlady sounded affronted. "That's when I go to bed."

"Of course," Tracey said soothingly. "And I hope to be back by then, but I'm not sure I can make it. Could I borrow a key?"

Mrs. Lester didn't look happy, but she finally nodded and took a key from the drawer of the hall table. "I'll have to charge you for this if you lose it."

"I understand." Tracey zipped it carefully into her purse. "I'll be very quiet when I come in, if it's late."

"That's all right, love. I'll leave a packet of sandwiches on the table if you like. There's a small charge, but you can have mackerel paste or chicken-and-salami paste with peppers."

Tracey almost shuddered visibly. Thank heaven,

she thought, the breakfast toast and eggs had come unadorned. Aloud she said, "I'll have a chance to eat dinner earlier, so it won't be necessary. Thanks all the same."

She escaped then, choosing to walk to the bus station through the town Common since it wasn't any great distance and the fresh morning air felt like a tonic. A few fortunate Southampton dogs were cavorting over the thick grass and around the flower-beds there, clearly enjoying their freedom from leashes carried by their owners. A Yorkshire terrier trotted along beside her for a few minutes before he dashed off to socialize with a friendly spaniel.

Tracey finally crossed the wide street bordering the Common and window-shopped as she walked through the center of town until she reached the station. Several men at the coffee bar there smiled while she waited for the next bus to Winchester, but she blandly ignored them, reading headlines at the newsstand to pass the time.

A few minutes later she had a seat to herself on the double-decker bus when it pulled out.

The road to Winchester went through a pleasant rolling countryside where rhododendrons and honey-suckle bordered large homes on either side. The houses were mainly of brick with tile roofs, spacious family dwellings where prams and bicycles were parked on the front porches. No one would have mistaken it for a road through an American suburb though. There were boxes labeled "grit" at the edge of the highway and "sale-agreed" signs on some of the brick houses. The flowerbeds of snapdragons and clematis might resemble their North American cousins but alongside there were "farm shops" instead of produce stands, and "tuck shops" instead of confectioneries. The "neighborhood news agent" was next door to a bicycle shop which advertised "spares." Nevertheless, there was an air of normalcy about it all and Tracey relaxed, trying to forget about her coming evening at Ardsley House.

A little later, when the bus came into a busy city with impressive outlines of a magnificent cathedral—the longest Gothic church in the world—there was no doubt that she'd arrived at Winchester.

For the next few hours Tracey wandered happily around the picturesque town, enjoying the many quaint old gates and houses. She saved the cathedral for the last of her sightseeing and enjoyed every part of the famous building, from the intricately carved choir stalls to the impressive vaulted ceiling. She noted Jane Austen's grave along with the statue to St. Joan of Arc and then slowly made her way back through to the nave with its soaring arches and pillars.

When she walked outside into the sunlight again after viewing all the historical riches, it was like coming back to another era. And then modern-day reality triumphed as she realized that it was early afternoon and her empty midsection told her that lunch was overdue.

She found a stucco-fronted pub with a chalkboard by the door advertising roast beef as the daily special. After going inside, she found to her delight that the roast beef was accompanied by creamed potatoes, Yorkshire pudding, string beans, and delicious hot coffee. It was the best meal she'd had since Bart had squired her around London. She lingered over the coffee, resting after her sightseeing and enjoying the classical music the bartender had on the radio.

Remembrance of her lunch with Bart brought back the guilt feelings she'd been trying to submerge ever since she'd hung up on him the night before. Now that she analyzed her behavior, she knew that stubborn feminine pride was the only reason she'd been so secretive about where she was staying. The sensible thing would be to seek Bart out right after she reported to Ardsley. He would realize that there was nothing wrong in her presence there—especially if she simply waited table at the Elizabethan banquet and kept her eyes open.

She felt much better about life in general once she'd made that resolve, and had another cup of coffee on the strength of it. Afterward she wandered across the grass of the churchyard for a look at the famed headstone of Thomas Thetcher before she walked back to the bus station. She smiled wryly at the sixteenth-century verse which started "Here sleeps in peace a Hampshire Grenadier, who caught his death by drinking cold small beer," and a few minutes later she strolled down the main cinder path toward the street.

She didn't hurry, knowing that she had allowed just about the right amount of time to get back to Southampton on one of the frequent buses. She walked behind a couple with two young children until one of the toddlers fell flat and burst into angry tears. While he was being soothed by his mother, Tracey waited—reluctant to force her way through the family group, which was taking up most of the path just then.

Her gaze moved absently out to the street and was attracted to a bright-colored sports car parked at the curb. Tracey recalled vaguely that there had been a similar car in the garages at Ardsley. Her eyes

widened then as she recognized the man who got out
from behind the steering wheel to wait by the car. It
wasn't fair that Bart could excel as such a prime ex-
ample of masculinity, Tracey thought, and sighed
unconsciously. There was no disguising the width of
his impressive shoulders in his blazer or the firm
lean line of his jaw, even from her profile glimpse.
He was staring along another path leading to the
main entrance of the cathedral, but Tracey stepped
back instinctively. A moment later she discovered
that she needn't have worried about being recognized. All of Bart's attention just then was on Stella
Frome, who was hurrying down the main path
toward him. Once she reached him, she threw her
arms around his neck and pulled his head down to
her laughing face.

Tracey didn't wait to see any more. She turned
blindly and hurried across the churchyard to find another route back to the center of town. To think that
she'd been tempted to bare her soul to the man as
soon as she reached Ardsley! Tracey kicked a stone
at the edge of the path, wishing that it was a convenient part of Bart's derriere instead.

She thrust her hands into her jacket pockets and
went on, keeping her gaze on the walk in front of
her. The shop windows to her right might as well
have been invisible for the attention she gave them;
instead all her thoughts were occupied with Stella
Frome's happy face as she'd raised her lips to Bart in
that scene beside the car.

Dammit to hell! Tracey thought as she trudged
along. With all the British Isles at their disposal,
why couldn't the two of them find another part of
the countryside instead of dogging her footsteps? Of
course, she told herself, there was a traditional rea-

son for couples visiting church rectors, and from Stella's ecstatic expression, the mission was successful.

Tracey clenched her teeth so tightly that her jaw ached as she strode down the sidewalk. She'd have one night at Ardsley, she promised herself. If she didn't turn up anything interesting on that miserable worktable in the storage room, she'd abandon the whole idea. Tomorrow she'd go back to London and see how soon she could get a plane reservation home. As far as Bart was concerned, she'd phone a farewell message to his London hotel from the airport.

She was busily composing what she'd say in the terse message on the bus ride back to Southampton. The bus conductor gave her white, unhappy countenance a worried look as he came to collect her fare. Normally he would have lingered to pass the time of day with such an attractive passenger, but as soon as Tracey received her change, she stared fixedly out the bus window again. He looked slightly annoyed before he shrugged and pulled the bell cord, signaling the driver to move on. A man couldn't win them all, he decided philosophically.

Tracey remained unaware of the conductor's decision, indeed of his very existence, as the bus retraced its route to Southampton.

She got off at the main terminal and walked around to the taxi rank at the street, where a cab was waiting. The driver appeared delighted to pick up a fare going to the New Forest on what was evidently a quiet afternoon as far as customers were concerned.

Tracey's preoccupied expression must have shown the man that she wasn't in the mood for idle conversation, and aside from a desultory comment on the improved weather, they made the entire trip in silence.

She asked him to let her out near the staff entrance when they finally reached the curving drive to Ardsley House. The big manor house looked almost ethereal in the gathering dusk of the late afternoon, so unreal that Tracey wouldn't have been surprised to find a ducal barouche waiting at the main entrance or a uniformed footman standing on the broad stone steps.

It was almost a relief to see Mrs. Jenks' solid figure when she opened her door to Tracey's knock. The housekeeper looked more dignified than before, in her short black taffeta dress.

"Well, it's nice to find someone these days who comes to work on time," she said, giving Tracey an approving glance. "You're even a mite early, but I hope you don't mind starting right in. Have you had your tea?"

"I'm not a bit hungry." Tracey didn't have to stretch the truth on that. Ever since she'd seen Bart at Winchester, the thought of food hadn't occurred to her. "I had a late lunch," she went on when Mrs. Jenks frowned with indecision.

"Mind you, it's going to be a long night," the housekeeper said slowly. "You wouldn't believe how many steps you have to take between the kitchen and the banquet hall. That's why it's so hard to keep any permanent help here."

"I promise I'll let you know if malnutrition sets in," Tracey assured her.

"All right, then. I'd like you to start setting some of the tables. You can get into your costume afterward—otherwise, you're apt to get chilled. It's hard to get enough heat in that barn of a room when it's just used three times a week. I'll find a dress for you in the meantime." Her appraising glance went over Tracey's figure. "Come back in here and change just before it's time to serve."

"Will my shoes be all right?"

Mrs. Jenks surveyed Tracey's blue pumps and nodded. "Just so they're comfortable. The color doesn't matter, because the long skirt will hide them. Actually, the dress is a brown-and-blue chintz, so it should go nicely. Leave your purse over here in my desk drawer and I'll lock it up. I'll get it out for you when you leave."

Since the purse contained most of Tracey's traveler's checks and her passport, she was glad to stash it in a safe place. Whatever else was going on at Ardsley, Mrs. Jenks appeared to be the soul of integrity.

She was also efficient and a dynamo at organization. Tracey was taken on a lightning tour of the big kitchen, where three women were already busy over mammoth aluminum kettles at the long stove and a younger helper was filling glass dishes with fruit cocktail. After a general round of introductions, Mrs. Jenks motioned Tracey to follow her. This time, it was along a corridor with brown linoleum on the floor, where overhead lights were casting a feeble glow. "Nobody ever wanted to make any improvements on the staff quarters," Mrs. Jenks tossed over her shoulder as she bowled along. "And now Mr. Oliver has so many places to spend money that the poor man hardly knows what to do first. It isn't as if he doesn't try," she added loyally. "Now, this is where you'll spend most of your time. It's a lovely room, isn't it? Quite one of the nicest in this wing."

A British understatement if there ever was one,

Tracey thought. The dining hall was immense and the magnificent oak paneling on its walls must have been worth a fortune in itself. There was also a tremendous marble-fronted fireplace on one side with what seemed to be small trees stacked in it for the banquet blaze. Overhead there were silver chandeliers which had been converted to electricity but were still incredibly ornate. Tracey decided that polishing Ardsley silver in that room alone could take weeks, and gave silent thanks that she was only temporary help.

There had been no attempt to use authentic furnishings for the evening's banquet. Instead, there were long folding tables, obviously put up for the occasion and covered with serviceable dark red cloths. "They don't show the soil so badly," Mrs. Jenks said, seeing the direction of Tracey's glance. "We rent the flatware, too." She gestured toward big boxes full of cutlery which were stacked on a table by the door. "Some visitors like to use their fingers—all their lives they've read about Henry VIII eating chicken that way and think this is the time to try it. That's why we have the finger bowls," she added, jerking her head toward stacks of containers that had the look of pewter. "One man actually wanted us to furnish a dog with a thick coat for a serviette. Imagine! Just because he'd seen it at the cinema."

Tracey grinned sympathetically and hoped that it hadn't been an American who'd wanted the canine napkin.

Mrs. Jenks was going on. "You'd think people would know better, but just because they've bought a ticket they think they can act like a bunch of teddy boys. Mr. Oliver says we just have to close our eyes to such things. It's easy for him—he isn't here most of the time."

"Will he be here tonight?" Tracey slipped the question in casually.

"Yes, indeed! He's ordered dinner in the family quarters at seven for him and his guests. Sometimes he comes down to supervise the entertainment." Seeing Tracey's puzzled expression, she added, "The singers and the young men from the village who play recorders and lutes."

"It sounds very nice."

Mrs. Jenks pursed her lips and nodded. "We think so. Nigel organized the 'do'—he's Mr. Oliver's manager. Has a finger in most everything."

"Does he attend the banquet, too?" It was hard for Tracey to keep her voice uncaring on that, but she made a stab at it.

"He's usually around keeping track of things." Mrs. Jenks' expression sharpened. "Why? Do you know him?"

"No." Tracey waved a vague hand. "Your nephew must have mentioned his name. When he was telling me about Ardsley."

"It's just as well. Our Nigel—Mr. Pelham, that is—fancies himself as a ladies' man." She bit her lip as if wondering how much more she should say.

"I'm already spoken for"—Tracey made her tone airy—"so he'll have to try his luck somewhere else."

"It's better that way. I think you had best start fixing these tables first off. The place setting should look like this," the housekeeper said, getting out some of the cutlery. "Afterwards you can put a folded serviette at each place and a finger bowl in front. You'll have to carry water from the kitchen to fill the bowls, but at least it can be done ahead of time. Once you're finished with that, you'd better change into your serving dress. If I'm not in the kitchen, just go on in my apartment. I'll leave one or two dresses on the sofa, and you can choose the one that fits best. Any questions?"

Tracey shook her head.

"Good girl," Mrs. Jenks said, nodding approvingly. "Cook can help you out on most problems. Remember, everything has to be ready in here by seven-fifteen sharp. That's when the buses bring the people."

The intervening time sped by faster than Tracey could have imagined. It seemed that she'd no sooner finished setting the long tables than she was putting baskets of rolls down the center and placing pewter-type mugs in readiness for the ale which was to come later. There were others in the crew getting things ready; two men brought risers and chairs for the musicians in the gallery at one end of the big room, and an elderly man methodically wheeled in stacks of folding chairs. There was even a sound system to be tested, and Tracey grinned at that. Apparently the soft strains of Elizabethan music from the gallery couldn't compete with the conversational din expected from the floor.

She reached a stopping place in her tasks a half-hour before the first guests were expected and was urged by the friendly kitchen crew to "have a cuppa" before she changed.

Tracey accepted, glad of a chance to sit down in a corner of the big room out of the way and sip steaming tea with one of the banquet rolls and butter. She watched Oliver Rustad's dinner, and presumably Bart's and Stella's, wheeled down the long corridor toward the dining hall during the interval. The family quarters, she was told, were in the same wing only a little farther on.

If Oliver Rustad was feeling a financial pinch, it wasn't evident in his menu. There were mammoth silver trays containing Dover sole for the fish course and a mouth-watering rack of lamb surrounded by fresh vegetables to follow. Tracey saw another waiter carefully carrying three bottles of wine and stemmed glasses banded in gold. Finally there was a trolley with the "sweet," as Ardsley's cook called it—a banana-and-custard-chiffon flan on a crystal pedestal. The desert looked utterly delicious and contained enough calories for an entire village. Tracey watched it go by and suddenly scowled down at the remnants of her roll and butter. It was no wonder that Marie Antoinette hadn't endeared herself to the populace of France—probably the cake she'd popularized had looked a lot like that banana flan.

Tracey swallowed a last bite of roll and carried her dishes to the counter by the big sink, carefully dodging the busy kitchen help. Mrs. Jenks wasn't in evidence, so she walked on down to the housekeeper's apartment as she'd been told and let herself in after a tentative knock on the door.

The living room was unoccupied, but Mrs. Jenks had left two long chintz dresses and a ruffled mobcap on the crocheted afghan covering the sofa. Tracey went over and held up one of the dresses, biting her lip in dismay as she saw the style. Evidently the bodice had been designed by someone who thought serving wenches spent as much time in the bedroom as the dining room. There was precious little material, and an off-the-shoulder ruffle had to double as a sleeve. The ruffle was repeated at the bottom of the dress, which turned demure as the skirt reached her ankles.

Tracey went over and locked the housekeeper's door before changing and then checked her appearance in a mirror afterward. It was no wonder that Mrs. Jenks complained about the behavior of the male banquet guests. The ruffled mobcap on her blond hair made Tracey look like some Victorian parlor maid who spent most of her time in the butler's pantry, while the dress gave the impression that she was part of the feast.

Suddenly it occurred to her that she shouldn't be standing around the housekeeper's quarters when there was probably work for her to do in the dining hall. She left her own clothes in a neatly folded pile at the end of the sofa and went out of the apartment, closing the door behind her.

For an instant she was tempted to detour by the storage room and see if it had been left unlocked, but another glance at her watch made her realize the futility of that idea. In five minutes there'd be an organized search party if she didn't appear in the kitchen. She'd just have to manage to miss the bus back to town after the banquet and make her explorations when the house quieted down for the night.

As she hurried back to the kitchen, Tracey felt a moment's disquiet at the thought of such nocturnal wanderings. Not only that, finding a way back to Southampton in the middle of the night was hardly a cheery prospect. It would have been far easier if she'd managed to work out a partnership with Bart rather than do it on her own. Unfortunately, from the look on his face at Winchester, he'd been thinking about more pleasant types of reconnaissance.

Mrs. Jenks met Tracey as soon as she set foot in

the kitchen and commented, "You look ready to take off somebody's head. Those tourists haven't been getting at you already, have they?"

"No. I just got changed," Tracey replied. She restrained an impulse to yank up her bodice after one of the musicians audibly smacked his lips as he wandered by on his way to the banqueting hall. "You're sure this is the waitress's uniform?" she asked Mrs. Jenks when he'd gone past.

The older woman looked slightly embarrassed. "It's certainly not what I would have chosen. Just be careful when you lean over with the plates. On second thought, maybe you should pour the ale at the serving section and let the others work at the tables. Afterwards, you can wheel the trolleys back to the kitchen when they clear. That's just before the entertainment starts. You'll miss most of the tips, but—"

"That doesn't matter," Tracey said hastily. "Thank you. I'd rather stay in the background."

"In that outfit, I don't think you'll be ignored even there, but it should help," the housekeeper said. "Get along, now. You'll be kept busy with the ale—it's served all through the meal."

Tracey had reason to be grateful for Mrs. Jenks' foresight. The guests filling the huge banqueting hall were determined to get their money's worth, one way or another. As the meal progressed and the ale goblets were drained again and again, the banquet noise was almost beyond belief. The temperature rose, too, with a blaze crackling in the huge fireplace. The nearby guests started using their napkins as fans or dipped them into their finger bowls and cooled their hot faces that way. For the first time, Tracey felt happy with her serving dress—especially since she'd managed to drape a muslin dish towel over her shoulders so the position of her bodice ruffle wasn't quite so critical. At least she didn't have to check it every time she bent over a pitcher. There had been two male guests, overflowing with *joie de vivre*, who'd sidled up to her table. One had left reluctantly when she'd smiled and said *"Ich verstehe nicht"* and then *"Non capisco"* when he'd asked what she was doing for the rest of the night. The other man left much faster when she happened to drop a mug of ale down the leg of his jeans. Mrs. Jenks sailed past when that happened and winked at Tracey before mopping up the young man and escorting him back to his table.

There was a lull after that episode, and Tracey leaned back against the paneled wall to catch her breath while the guests were making inroads on a champagne ice. Her glance wandered to the musicians' gallery, where the chorus was assembling, and she caught a profile glimpse of three men. One was Oliver Rustad, but it was Bart's tall, dark-haired figure beside him which was distressingly familiar—even in that brief glance before she looked down again in panic.

If Bart had been surveying the scene long, there wasn't any doubt that he'd recognized her, probably even seen her cool off her ardent admirer with the ale. On the other hand, he might only have seen the mobcap as she bent over the table. There wasn't much chance he'd say anything to his host, and Oliver Rustad certainly wouldn't identify her from one chance meeting on the path at Beaulieu.

It was the presence of that third man which brought a frown to her face. If Nigel Pelham had recognized her, surely he wouldn't be able to do much about it until the banquet was over. Especially since the entertainment would soon be going at full tilt.

Tracey looked around the room and noticed that Mrs. Jenks had disappeared again. The women working at the tables were just starting to clear the final course, and there were plenty of waiters to get the dishes back to the kitchen. Without trying to rationalize any further, Tracey slipped from the banquet hall into the kitchen corridor.

The kitchen itself was almost deserted. There were only two women rinsing serving platters at the big sink, and Tracey walked quickly through the other side of the room without attracting their attention. She hurried into the deserted corridor leading to Mrs. Jenks' apartment, feeling as if she'd absconded with the banquet cash box.

Which was silly, because all she wanted to do was change her clothes and see if she could find any way to get in that storage room where the worktable was stored before Nigel Pelham arrived—intent on renewing their acquaintance.

Tracey gave an involuntary shudder and looked over her shoulder as she tapped on Mrs. Jenks' door, letting herself in when there was no response to her knock.

She looked swiftly round the woman's living room and searched her adjoining bedroom and bath to make sure there was no one in the apartment. Only then did she carefully latch the hall door and start to change out of her serving dress.

It was the key ring left atop the nearby desk which stopped her before she'd even touched the side zipper. She walked over to the desktop and picked up the heavy keys, staring down at them thoughtfully. Mrs. Jenks must have been so caught up with the banquet activities that she'd simply walked off and forgotten them. Either that or she hadn't wanted to wear the bulky key ring at her waist on such a festive evening. Whatever the reason, it was a minor miracle as far as Tracey was concerned.

Her fingers were trembling as she let herself out of the apartment, carefully clutching the key ring at her side. The corridor was still deserted, and she didn't waste any time making her way to the storeroom where she'd seen the worktable earlier.

It took longer than she liked to find the proper key for the heavy wooden door, and Tracey nearly collapsed with fright at one point when she heard voices and footsteps on the gravel drive outside. She drew in her breath sharply and flattened herself against the wall, hoping that whoever it was wouldn't come in.

The footsteps became progressively fainter, and Tracey exhaled slowly, sure that she'd aged five years in the interval. Then she shook herself mentally; the only people apt to be interested in what she was doing were Mrs. Jenks, Nigel, and possibly Bart. And since she wasn't sure that the latter two even suspected she was wandering around, there was no point having a nervous breakdown just then.

Her logic must have had some effect, because the next key on Mrs. Jenks' ring clicked easily in the lock and the storeroom door swung inward.

"Hallelujah!" Tracey breathed fervently, and stepped over the threshold into the darkened room. Before she shut the hall door behind her, she glanced around to see if there was any way that she could curtain the windows and be able to turn on the overhead light. Unfortunately, there weren't any drapes, but she did see a small flashlight on top of a bookcase nearby.

She walked across and picked it up, checking to make sure the feeble beam worked before going back to close the hall door. For an instant she debated leaving the housekeeper's key ring on the inside of the lock and then decided against it, dropping it instead in the deep pocket on the side of her skirt. It was so heavy that she felt like a boat listing in a storm afterward, but at least it was safe for the moment.

She didn't waste any more time after that. There was enough moonlight shining through the mullioned windows that she could see the outlines of the stored furniture, making her investigation easier. She twisted through the pieces as carefully as she could, trying not to dislodge the muslin dustcovers tossed over some or the newspapers which were even more casually piled atop others. When she flashed her light about, she took care to keep the beam as low as possible in case someone might be walking on the path outside. For the first time, it occurred to her that the whole setup might be her imagination, that the worktable she'd seen in London had been genuine and that the ridiculous price had simply been a mistake—one that had been corrected as soon as Oliver Rustad had heard what was happening to his belongings.

Tracey grimaced as she thought about it. If that were the case, what in the deuce was she doing breaking into a locked room? More than likely she'd be a candidate for the Southampton jail if Mrs. Jenks returned for her keys and instituted a search.

It was an almost overwhelming temptation to bolt

for the door and get back to the safety of the hall. In
a matter of minutes she could change into her own
clothes in the housekeeper's rooms and call for a taxi
to take her back to town.

The impulse was so strong that Tracey actually
started toward the door before she caught herself.
There was no reason, she told herself sternly, that
she couldn't do all those things *after* she'd checked
out the worktable. That way, she would have accomplished everything she set out to do.

If she'd been honest, she would have admitted
that an urge to score over Bart was the deciding factor. Feminine pride rebelled at having to go back
and eventually admit to him that she hadn't learned
one damned thing except how to fill ale flagons at
an Elizabethan banquet!

Strengthened by that resolve, Tracey made her
way to the small piece of furniture by the window,
which she'd vaguely identified the day before. She
hesitated when she saw that a muslin covering had
been draped over it in the interval. Was it possible
that she was already too late? That the worktable
had been shifted earlier or that she'd somehow broken into the wrong room?

She had to put down her flashlight on a nearby
kneehole desk before she could remove the dustcover, but then she felt a surge of triumph at the
piece of furniture revealed. It was the same worktable she'd seen at the antique mart in Kensington
High Street—she'd bet her salary on it.

Swiftly she dropped to her knees in front of the
Regency piece to check it out. Then she muttered in
exasperation and stood up to get the flashlight again.
Determining the authenticity of an antique was diffi-

cult even under ideal conditions. Tracey wouldn't have qualified as an expert if she'd had everything going for her, but at least she knew enough to check the more obvious indications of forgery.

Pulling out the short drawer under the rectangular top, she bent over to flash her light on the board at the back of it. She really didn't expect to find any crude mistakes such as the mark of a band saw, but it wouldn't have been the first time such fakery had been tried. The drawer looked to be genuine, and she replaced it carefully after checking to see if the wood on the front had been replaced. After that, she scrutinized the hardware on the keyhole for authenticity as well. Tracey directed the flashlight beam onto the wood of the base, making sure the finish matched the upper part of the table—that it hadn't been "married" to the other section in a common practice where Regency tops sometimes acquired a genuine Edwardian bottom.

Tracey went over all the details she could remember and then sat back on her heels and considered the worktable through narrowed eyes. The piece looked wonderful—it was in tip-top condition, and at the price Nigel Pelham had quoted to her in Kensington, it had been a real steal. Which was exactly what it was, she decided. Somehow it had gotten to Kensington, ostensibly without Oliver Rustad's knowledge. Then, just as quickly, it had been withdrawn. All of which proved exactly nothing, Tracey thought confusedly as she got to her feet.

She was so intent on her thoughts that she didn't take sufficient care when she threaded her way back through the furniture toward the door. Her full skirt brushed a pile of newspapers which were care-

lessly stacked against the edge of a Georgian bureau
cabinet and sent them slithering to the floor, taking
the muslin dustcover from another piece of furniture with them.

"Damn it to . . ." Tracey's exasperated ut-
terance broke off as she flashed the light over the
chaos and its beam rested squarely on a faithful du-
plicate of the first mahogany worktable. Tracey's
mouth dropped open and then closed slowly. So
much for her expert appraisal! She wondered giddily
how many more worktables Nigel or his boss had
stashed away in Ardsley, waiting to be unleashed on
the gullible public.

Well, there was no point just standing there be-
moaning such a shabby shocker, she decided at last.
The thing to do was get out and tell somebody
about it—somebody like Bart, who would know the
next step to take.

She'd just turned toward the hall when approaching footsteps coming down the corridor made
her freeze in horror. A moment later, there was the
rattle of a key in the door.

Tracey drew an uneven breath and looked around
the shadowed room desperately. She just had time to
notice that she'd left the flashlight atop another
muslin cover when the person at the door belatedly
discovered that he'd been locking an unlocked door
instead of the other way around. The key snicked in
the lock again and then the door flew open with an
angry shove.

Nigel's figure on the threshold of the room was
plainly visible from the overhead hall light behind
him. His eyebrows came together in a black ominous
line as he stared in at the tumbled mess of newspa-

per on the floor and the second worktable in plain view without its cover. Then he growled, "Bloody hell!" like an omen of things to come and stepped into the room.

9

When Tracey saw the door close behind him, she felt a wave of sheer terror. By then she was bent double in the center of the kneehole desk, only partially hidden by a trailing end of muslin. She knew her cover wouldn't last if Nigel decided to search the premises, and she had almost decided to make a break for the door when he found the flashlight she'd left. He directed its beam onto the second worktable she'd uncovered, muttering something incredibly profane as he shrouded it with muslin again. An instant later he flashed the light over the spilled newspapers, but he merely kicked the top ones out of his way as he walked swiftly back to the hall door and went out into the corridor again.

Tracey stayed where she was, scarcely daring to breathe. There was no mistaking the sound of Nigel's key in the lock as he secured the door behind him. Obviously he'd decided that whoever had gotten into the room had left long before. The fact that she'd neglected to lock the door behind her had turned out to be a stroke of genius. At least it had convinced him the intruder had fled. On the other hand, if she'd locked the door, he might have thought that the papers had simply slithered over by themselves and uncovered the table.

Well, it was too late to change anything now, she acknowledged, and crawled out from under the desk. She'd been so frightened that she'd scrunched herself into an impossible ball, and her muscles were protesting. She didn't waste time thinking about the aches, since what might have happened if Nigel had discovered her hiding place would have been far more painful.

She was still breathing like a distance runner when she tiptoed over to the door. She listened with her ear against the wood for a full minute before daring to reach in her skirt and pull out Mrs. Jenks' key ring. Then she took care to get the right key in the lock without allowing a telltale metallic clank from the rest of the bunch. If there'd been time, she would have given herself an accolade for keeping the keys in her pocket instead of leaving them on a tabletop along with the flashlight. Not that she'd planned it that way; she'd just been lucky.

Her nerves almost failed her when it came to opening the door and stepping out into the hallway. Unfortunately, the only alternative was sitting in the storage room and waiting for Nigel to reappear.

She inched the knob around with the care of a safecracker and managed to pull the door open without making any noise. A few seconds later, when she poked her head past the jamb, she felt like William Tell waiting for the first arrow. It wasn't until a second or two later that she realized she'd closed her eyes in the maneuver. That had to be the most appalling thing she'd done yet, and she almost groaned aloud as she realized it.

Fortunately there was no one in the corridor to

view such inanity, and she slipped over the threshold, easing the door shut behind her. She hesitated then, wondering whether to head down the hall toward Mrs. Jenks' apartment or detour to the outside path.

The latter choice somehow seemed safer, and she moved quickly to the hall door, giving a relieved murmur when it opened under her fingers. She whisked around it safely, but a last look over her shoulder revealed Nigel turning into the hallway on a return visit.

It was the barest fleeting glimpse, because his reappearance spurred Tracey to instant flight. She abandoned any thoughts of the path, ducking instead under the heavy branches of the rhododendrons planted against the walls of Ardsley.

After estimating how long it would take Nigel to reach the doorway behind her, she suddenly crouched down in the thick of the greenery and waited. If Nigel followed her into the shrubs, she'd break out into the open and try for the parked tour buses by the Hall's main entrance. The drivers might be waiting outside and give her refuge.

The next few seconds seemed interminable because Nigel was apparently using the same tactics of silence. The branches of the rhododendrons blocked out her view, so she could only hope that he was still on the path, trying to locate her.

After what seemed an eternity, she heard footsteps hurrying the other way, finally to disappear as he left the path. Evidently he was going to search the outbuildings by the staff quarters.

Of course, he didn't have any real reason to suspect that she was even connected with the storage room, Tracey rationalized as she got to her feet and pushed on through the shrubs toward Ardsley's main entrance. Her thudding heart told her not to count on such fool logic; if Nigel Pelham hadn't given a damn, he certainly wouldn't be moving as fast as he was now.

By then, Tracey had reached the curving flower-beds next to Ardsley's stone steps. A frantic glance around disclosed that the forecourt of the estate was deserted. Apparently English tour drivers went in to sensibly drink tea or watch the musical entertainment rather than wait outside in a chilly bus.

Tracey didn't realize how cold it was until she automatically brushed a twig from her sleeve ruffle and found that her skin was icy to the touch. One shiver coursed through her body, and then another. She'd have to get inside fast or end up in the pneumonia ward of the local hospital.

She judged the distance across the open grounds to the entrance and decided to make a dash for it. It wasn't until she was halfway up the broad steps that she wondered if those thick doors were unlocked. God help her if she had to stand outside pounding on them for admission, and that would be the case, because there certainly wasn't anything on Mrs. Jenks' key ring to fit them.

Tracey grasped the heavy wrought-iron handle on a portal that could have belonged to a Plantagenet king. Disdaining any social niceties, she shoved with all her might and almost fell full-length when the door opened smoothly. Fortunately there was no one around to observe her struggling to regain her balance. The faint sounds of music in the distance showed the banquet program must still be in full swing and occupying most of the household.

Probably Bart would be there, too, Tracey reasoned as she closed the heavy door behind her with a satisfying thud. Then she caught sight of herself in an antique smoked mirror at the side of the entranceway and almost moaned aloud. It was a good thing there *wasn't* anyone around. Her Elizabethan serving dress didn't have much to recommend it in the first place, and it certainly had a lot less now. Climbing through the shrubbery hadn't been on the designer's list of suggested activities; the ruffle drooped in torn disarray and the skirt was stained with green mold from the rhododendrons.

The faint impulse she'd had to check out the banquet guests died aborning. She'd have to find something else to wear right away before she was discovered looking like some serving wench who'd been tumbled in the flowerbed instead of the hay.

An appraisal of the barnlike drawing room which loomed in front of her showed that she'd have to search for wearing apparel in another part of the wing. There was enough upholstered furniture on the waxed parquet floor to stock a store, but nothing so much as a throw over a sofa to improve her costume. She would have liked to go over and warm herself in front of the fireplace blaze, but she didn't dare linger. Instead, she turned to a curved stair at her right, which led to the upper stories.

It would have been better if she'd done some exploring earlier, she thought as she hurried up the worn but polished treads. Just then she had to hope that she'd find an unoccupied bedroom with a closet full of clothes. Later, she could reclaim her own things.

The stairway ended in a wide hallway which evidently paralleled the front of Ardsley, with doors opening off to her right. That meant the rooms must overlook the gardens and fountain on the other side, she reasoned. As she tiptoed down the hall toward the first doorway, she suddenly heard a male voice coming from what appeared to be another stairway at the far end of the corridor. She sprinted the last few feet to the door and reached for the knob, uttering a silent prayer that it wasn't locked.

After that, things happened so fast that she didn't know what came first. She *did* know that, as the door opened, a masculine arm emerged to yank her inside. The door closed behind her even as she opened her mouth to protest, but a hand clamped over her lips before she could utter a sound. An instant later she was staring with frightened eyes up into Bart Jennings' angry face. Before that shock registered fully, she remembered hearing Nigel's voice from the other stairs moments before. Almost desperately she tore Bart's hand away to hiss, "There isn't time to explain—I have to hide. Nigel's out there looking for me."

Bart pulled her back again when she started for the center of his bedroom. "What do you mean? What's going on?"

She yanked her arm loose. "Don't argue! He knows I've been in the storeroom. I saw two of those work-tables—lord knows how many more he's stashed in the place." Her glance was going round the chamber as her words tumbled out. She noted an imposing armoire which stood against the paneled wall and then focused on the huge four-poster bed with its silk canopy and hangings. "I can hide under that bed. There'd be room for a regiment—" Her voice broke as they both heard the angry slam of a door nearby.

Bart's furious expression became even more pronounced as he eyed Tracey's disreputable gown. "Damned if you don't deserve what you're going to get. Come here!" He towed her across the expanse of oak flooring to the bed like an irate parent with a recalcitrant child. Without a wasted gesture, he shoved her down on the blanket atop it and held her there. With his other hand he pulled off her blond wig, as if it offended him even more than she did.

"What in the devil do you think you're doing?" she got out, struggling furiously to sit upright and not getting anywhere against his arm, which kept her pinned to the bed.

"I'm trying to save your neck—although I'd rather wring it right now. Lie down and keep quiet!" The last warning came as he looked at her in lightning calculation and repositioned her on the bed like a stage director so that she was partially hidden behind the side hangings. Then, without displaying a sign of emotion, he reached over and tore her bedraggled bodice open all the way to her waist. An instant later he threw himself on the bed beside her, covering part of her upper body.

"Bart! No . . ." Tracey moaned in distress. "Don't—please—"

She knew that her soft protests wouldn't have convinced anyone. In truth, she was hardly aware that she made them. All that penetrated her being just then was the feel of his strong hand moving roughly, sensuously over her—arousing feelings in her body that she'd only guessed at before.

"Why not?" Bart's voice was deep with definite overtones of masculine triumph. "You can't blame me for wanting to look at you—to kiss every lovely inch of you." There was a pulsing interval while he bent over her—then he went on roughly, "This is the way it should be when a man makes love to a woman."

A metallic click from the doorway punctuated the end of his sentence. Tracey's eyes widened in shock, but Bart remained where he was beside her. His hand came back from its exploring forays on her soft skin, moving up to her shoulder to keep her immobile on the bed.

He needn't have bothered with the precaution; Tracey couldn't have moved a muscle at that moment if her life had depended on it. All the fabled feelings of maidenly modesty—the strictures of lady-like behavior—had vanished from her thoughts when he'd first touched her. And when his dark-eyed glance had wandered possessively over her, her instinctive impulse was to pull him closer still.

It was the paralyzing stillness in the room that penetrated her consciousness. When she finally whispered, "Bart—what is it?" he pushed up on an elbow and moved away.

"I think he's gone," he answered ruefully. "That little scene must have convinced him. At least enough not to break in and ask questions." Seeing her still-dazed expression, he added, "Your friend Nigel. I sincerely hope that's who opened the door—I couldn't take a chance on checking just then. You don't have to worry—the only glimpse he got of you was a bare shoulder, if I figured out the logistics properly."

"Logistics!" Tracey felt a betraying flood of color washing over her. All the time he was staging a diversion, she'd been fool enough to think he meant it!

Bart grimaced as he heard the scorn in her voice. He started to help her pull part of the bedspread over her, and then stopped, not even rolling away so that she could grasp the spare material.

Tracey made no attempt to hide her fury at that. "Do you mind moving? That is, if 'Show and Tell' time is over now. It's hard to keep up with your devious plans!" She fumbled angrily with the edge of the heavy spread and managed to cover her breasts with it, but it was a precarious barrier. Her fingers yanked the satin higher as she struggled to sit upright.

"My plans!" he retorted, taken aback. "I like that."

"You seemed to at the time."

"That's gratitude for you. I suppose that I dragged you in here for some titillation. Is that it?"

"I don't know," she replied unhappily, knowing some of his anger was justified. "All I wanted to do was hide under the bed—not this."

"Oh, sure. With a few more brilliant ideas like that, you could have gotten us shot. What in the hell were you doing in the storeroom when he caught sight of you in the first place? No, don't tell me," he went on scathingly without giving her a chance to answer. "Let me guess. Probably taking flashbulb pictures for that damned article of yours."

"Don't be ridiculous! I didn't even have a camera," she replied, stung by his injustice. To think that she'd believed for one minute that he cared about her—that he'd really wanted to make love when she was in his arms. From the way he was acting now, he must be regretting every instance of that interval. Obviously it hadn't burned into his memory as the fulfillment of a cherished dream. Far from it!

At that moment, she wanted to crawl in the nearest corner and howl. Instead she had to stay clutching a miserable bedspread like somebody on a casting couch, trying to hide her wounded pride. "I wasn't crazy about wearing that dress of mine," she told him stiffly, "but it came with the job. Would you mind getting me something to replace it? This bedspread doesn't do a thing for me."

For the first time, the stern line of his jaw seemed to soften. "I don't know about that. You could do worse. Anyhow, there are more important things to take care of now." He resumed his brisk tone. "I have to let Oliver know what happened. I hope to God that you haven't put Nigel off with this latest caper of yours."

"Put him off? What are you talking about?"

"There isn't time to explain now—"

She flounced angrily, almost dislodging her covering in the process, but she was so annoyed that she didn't even care. "Dammit, don't say that again. I have a right to know what's going on—this was my idea in the first place."

"You're wrong there. It was apparently Nigel's brainchild, and he's been doing nicely with it for over a year now. I promise you that I'll explain later. You'll have to stay here out of sight for now, though. I hope to heaven he didn't recognize you when he peered in here." Bart stared worriedly at her for an instant. "That hair of yours is hard to hide, but with any luck, he wasn't concentrating on it. In fact," Bart went on softly with a wicked glint, "I doubt if your friend Nigel could even tell you his name when he finally closed that door."

"He's *not* my friend," Tracey retorted, her cheeks aflame. "And if you were any kind of a gentleman, you'd change the subject. Of course, a gentleman wouldn't have put me in this position in the first place."

"You may be a little short of clothes, but your head is still attached to your neck. Don't overlook that fact. Some women might appreciate it."

Tracey translated "some women" to mean Stella Frome, and the memory of their meeting in Winchester materialized again with discouraging accuracy. "Didn't you say something about having to leave?" she asked pointedly.

Bart had been admiring the silken sheen of her smooth skin in the lamplight, and he slid off the bed slowly. "Don't forget, you'll have to stay out of sight for a while. There's a robe of mine in the closet if you get tired of wearing that bedspread."

"Thanks very much, but I'll wait for my own things. They're in the housekeeper's apartment— Mrs. Jenks can bring them up."

Bart lingered by the bedroom door after reaching down to take the key from the lock. "You don't seem to understand," he said with terrible patience. "Right now, we're not advertising your presence. I thought you'd figured that out."

"I can follow the script, but I'd prefer to play my part with some clothes on. If Mrs. Jenks doesn't have time to fetch and carry, you can corral one of the waitresses from the banquet. They should be finished working by now."

"I'll see what I can do. There's a parlor maid who brings me cold cocoa at bedtime—"

"Whatever for?"

"Damned if I know. Something hot to drink, I suppose."

"Cold cocoa?" She was incredulous.

"I don't think it's cold when it leaves the kitchen.

Who cares? I pour it down the drain anyway." He lingered with his hand on the doorknob. "You'd better wedge a chair against this after I've locked it. There's probably more than one key floating around this place."

Tracey's cheeks paled slightly at that warning. No matter how much she resented his behavior, the thought of his leaving made her almost ill. "You won't be gone too long, will you?"

"Not any longer than I absolutely have to be. And this time—for God's sake—stay put!" He suddenly walked back to the edge of the bed where she was sitting. "I wish you'd stop looking at me like that," he said irritably.

"I didn't say a word," she protested weakly.

"I know." He reached over and pulled her up close against his chest, almost as if he couldn't help himself. "You're too damned beautiful—that's the trouble," he went on in a conversational tone as he stared down into her lovely gray-green eyes. "Even in a bedspread."

With that, he kissed her again. He took his time about it, and when she reluctantly relaxed against him, he gave a muffled growl of approval, parting her lips as the kiss deepened. Tracey's arms slipped around his body, enjoying the muscled strength of his back before her hands crept up to smooth his thick hair.

She had no idea how long it was before Bart pulled back from the embrace, bestowing a quick kiss on each of her hands as he brought them down from his shoulders. "Beautiful," he repeated softly, gazing down at her. "Absolutely beautiful."

Her bedspread had somehow come adrift during

the interval. He tucked it around her again with a curiously tender gesture before he walked back to the door and let himself out into the hall. An instant later she heard his key turn crisply in the lock.

10

Tracey absently clutched her bedspread as she went across to prop a chair under the doorknob, and then she walked slowly over to the closet to find the robe that Bart had mentioned. She didn't even look in a mirror until she'd wrapped the silken folds of navy blue around her. Then she confronted her reflection as if facing a stranger. Her auburn hair was ruffled, and Tracey shook her head bemusedly, unable to remember if Bart had run his hands through it. It was strange, because she recalled all too well the other places his hands had caressed her. She smiled, putting her fingers to her lips as if confirming another memory, and then walked across to sit in a petit-point chair in front of the fireplace.

All she had to do now, she told herself, was relax in front of the fire until her clothes arrived. Bart would probably be back a little later to tell her what had happened. It shouldn't be difficult for him to get a confession from Nigel—not if the manager had left many of his antique reproductions stored at Ardsley.

Tracey looked at her watch and compared it with a French clock on a marble-topped table nearby,

Only five minutes had elapsed since Bart had left. She got to her feet then and walked over to the diamond-paned windows flanked by velvet drapes, staring out into the darkness onto a fountain in the middle of the landscaped grounds. The moonlight put an ethereal aura around the fountain's bronze female figure, making it almost come alive in its lush surroundings. Probably it had been purchased by one of the later generations of Rustads, Tracey thought aimlessly. It didn't fit with the more stolid interior decor of Ardsley—certainly not with the paneled walls or beamed ceilings in the bedchamber. And there wasn't anything delicate about the four-poster where she'd lain in Bart's arms.

Restlessly Tracey turned and walked back across the room. Her glance lingered on the marble-topped bedside table and the cut velvet chair beyond. The room's furnishings were impressive but not altogether comfortable for an extended period of time. It was all very well for Bart to calmly go off and leave her there, Tracey told herself, but ever since the door had closed behind him, she'd felt increasingly guilty as the minutes passed.

She sat down absently on the side of the bed, and then, aware of where she was, she hastily got up again. To placate her guilt, she picked up the bedspread and smoothed it back neatly over the blanket. That way, the maid who came with her clothes wouldn't have any stories to relay to the housekeeper.

Not that she really cared about the household help, Tracey decided as she arranged the bolster pillows against the wall. It was Stella Frome's relationship with Bart which really worried her.

Bart might make a habit of bedroom flirtations in

English stately homes, and from the way Stella greeted him at Winchester, she appeared to be a very willing partner. Heaven only knew what had happened at Ardsley earlier during their stay. Bart could be making peace with the blond right then—to soothe his own conscience about deserting her earlier. He wouldn't have to give Tracey a second thought. He could tell himself that she made a habit of sleeping around. The newspapers were full of stories about the relaxed morals of modern women, and he probably thought she fit right into the role. Look at the way she'd submitted to him.

Tracey drew a deep breath as she recalled his masculine strength and appeal. All the man had to do was crook a finger and women would go down like ninepins. Unfortunately, there was no way she could admit such a thing without sounding silly and naive.

The clock on the table chimed the hour, and its thin, delicate notes pierced the chilling silence in the room. Tracey shivered suddenly, aware that the thin material of Bart's travel robe was no match against the falling temperature.

She walked back toward the fireplace, where the blaze had died down to glowing embers. On the way, she caught sight of the blond wig that Bart had yanked off her head earlier.

She picked it up in a sudden surge of temper and slammed it into the smoldering coals. It blazed briefly before disintegrating into ash.

As far as she was concerned, everything else was finished, as well. She stared grimly into the fireplace at the last remnants of her disguise and then moved over to remove the chair from under the doorknob. There was no doubt about the door being locked, but she even knelt to make sure his key hadn't been left in the lock. Bart hadn't overlooked a thing, it seemed.

That only left her the option of hammering on the door or shouting until someone in the household came to her assistance. She raised her palm to the wood, and then hesitated, lowering it again.

The trouble was, who would come if she called? Instinctively she knew that Bart wouldn't be lingering in the corridor. She'd feel an awful fool if Mrs. Jenks unlocked the door and discovered her in a guest's bathrobe. Tracey could scarcely claim that sitting around *sans* clothes was part of the evening's duties.

Or Stella might come along—and that would really be worse still. Of course, Tracey could always claim to have arrived together with the evening's refreshment, she thought, and sighed at the possibility. Just then, even lukewarm cocoa sounded marvelous.

"Damn and double damn!" she muttered, thinking it was a sad day when she was torn between dwelling on her unsatisfactory love life and wondering if she'd ever get anything to eat.

To take her mind off the food, she sat down again in one of the chairs next to the fire and noticed that Bart had left a book on Jacobean furniture on the cushion. At least she could look through it, she decided, to help pass the time.

The combination of warmth from the fire and the dry-as-dust text had her blinking sleepily before she'd finished a chapter. She tucked her feet up on the cushion beside her and settled more comfortably into a corner of the big upholstered chair, starting on chapter two.

When she opened her eyes, she was still staring at

the same page but the book had slid down into her lap and the clock on the table was chiming two.

By then she was too sleepy to do more than stumble across the room and check to see if the door were still locked. When she discovered that it was, it didn't seem as important as her discovery that the bed looked wonderfully comfortable. There was no point sitting in a chair when she could stretch out on that imposing four-poster. She cinched the belt on Bart's robe more tightly around her as she crawled under the blanket, and was soundly asleep by the time her head touched the pillow.

When a bloodcurdling screech roused her from slumber the next time, her thoughts were far more coherent. She'd toured enough stately homes to recognize the sound of a peacock probably strolling Ardsley's grounds, even before it came again. She relaxed and stretched luxuriously on the comfortable mattress of the four-poster. Oliver Rustad didn't stint when it came to modern-day amenities for his overnight guests. If she only had a cup of coffee for breakfast . . .

The thought of breakfast brought her bolt upright, and she switched on the bed lamp to check the clock across the room, whose dial showed five-thirty. She crossed to the window and pulled aside one of the thick drapes, looking out on another misty gray English morning. Beneath her, the smooth rolling lawn was silvery with dew, and the peacock strutting by the fountain lifted his feet high, as if disdainful of the soggy grass.

There wasn't any other sign of activity—the rest of the estate looked as if it had been asleep for centuries, with windows either shuttered or curtained.

For an instant Tracey wondered if she'd been

deserted completely. She realized how idiotic her suspicions, when she turned away from the window and saw that her clothes and purse from the housekeeper's room had been left neatly folded on a chair by the door. As she hurried across to check, she also discovered that the key had been replaced on the inside of the lock and that the bedroom door opened noiselessly to her touch.

She closed it again, deciding that Mrs. Jenks or a maid had been on duty earlier than she'd hoped. It had to be someone like that. If it had been Bart, he surely wouldn't have disappeared again without advising her of what had happened.

Or would he? Perhaps it had just been his diplomatic way of letting her know that her part in the proceedings was finished.

As Tracey finished dressing in the adjoining bathroom, she decided that was the only logical explanation. Her somber glance swept round the bath, which had obviously been converted from a walk-in closet by one of the Rustad owners for the convenience of his guests. Another modern convenience to be found in an English manor house. She could see the headline for her article in Oscar's magazine even then. If she stayed around, she could undoubtedly add some direct quotes from Ardsley's gracious owner—delivered over the breakfast table after Bart had finished explaining why she'd stayed at Ardsley overnight, even though uninvited. She could even see Stella's politely raised eyebrows when it all happened. And if the housekeeper caught sight of her, Tracey would be lucky to avoid having a plate of crumpets dumped in her lap.

Her obvious alternative was to simply disappear before the gathering of the clan at breakfast. That way, all the forced politeness and questioning looks could be avoided. Bart might be momentarily disconcerted, but there was no doubt in Tracey's mind that afterward he'd be grateful to be rid of her embarrassing and uninvited presence.

Tracey turned back the covers on the bed to air when she'd finished dressing and cast one last look around the bedroom. It wasn't really necessary. The scene with that four-poster bed would be engraved on her memory for the rest of her life.

The hallway outside the bedroom was deserted, and she moved cautiously into it, taking care to shut the door quietly behind her. With luck, she should be able to make her way out the front door without encountering any of the household staff. The kitchen windows overlooked another part of Ardsley's grounds, and unless the gardeners were working a dawn shift, she could reach the main road without being seen. After that, she'd try to hitch a ride back to Southampton or the nearest village.

She felt a tremor of uneasiness when she reached the main floor and shifted the bolt on the big front door. It creaked loudly enough to waken the family ghost, and Tracey stayed glued in place until she was sure that her action was undetected. Then she didn't waste any time pulling the door open and slipping out onto the stone porch.

She took a deep breath of the crisp morning air before walking briskly down the side of the graveled drive toward the road. If she tried to run, she certainly would attract attention. A purposeful walk should do the trick, she told herself, and tried to ignore a niggling impulse to turn around and shelter behind Ardsley's imposing doors once again.

Pride kept her from indulging in such a weak-kneed maneuver, but she felt relieved that she hadn't succumbed to temptation by the time she finally reached the hard-surfaced highway. Her hurried walk down the long drive had winded her, and she lingered on the shoulder of the road to rest before starting out again.

The sound of an automobile engine approaching brought her head up in sudden suspicion. She felt a moment of panic when she discovered that it was coming down the drive from Ardsley. Even as she looked for someplace to hide, she became aware that it was a nondescript little car that she'd never seen before. As it turned toward her, she realized that it was a made-to-order chance for her ride to town.

The driver must have been on the same wavelength, because he braked as she started to raise a thumb. She hurried over and pulled the door open when he stopped a few feet away. "Could you please give me a ride into the nearest . . ." Her question trailed off as she recognized the man behind the wheel.

Nigel Pelham reached across to catch her wrist and yank her into the seat beside him. "I'd be delighted to take you for a ride, Miss Winslow. In fact, I've been waiting all night to do just that."

11

"I must say that I didn't think you'd be stirring so early this morning," he went on conversationally. He kept a tight grip on her while he leaned across to close her door and then put the car in motion again. "From what I saw when I stuck my head in the bedroom last night, I thought Mr. Jennings would be keeping you on a very short leash." He managed a quick sideways glance to watch her cheeks redden. "What's the matter, love? Didn't he fancy you as a blond? Or was he afraid the high-and-mighty Stella would have had a go at you if you'd appeared at breakfast. She's not fond of competition."

Tracey's initial fright subsided somewhat as Nigel continued to talk. Apparently he had her tagged merely as one of Bart's *enamorada* and was thoroughly enjoying her discomfiture. He'd loosened his grip on her wrist, although he hadn't replaced his hand on the steering wheel. "It would be our luck to meet a friend of the boss in London," he was going on placidly. "If you'd just kept your mouth shut about the worktable, Herbie wouldn't have got in trouble—and you wouldn't be here now."

"Herbie?" Tracey tried to keep her voice as unconcerned as possible.

"Your chum from the sale at Piccadilly. The one who tipped you off about going to the Kensington Arcade in the first place."

Her shrug was a masterpiece of injured innocence. "Well, how was I to know that it was going to get you into trouble? Bart had never mentioned Ardsley or Oliver Rustad to me."

"I can well imagine. Probably doesn't waste a lot of his time talking when he's with you, eh?"

Tracey would liked to have wiped the leer from his face with the back of her hand, but his restraining grip made it impossible—even if she could have escaped afterward. He hadn't slackened speed on the road, which wound through what must have been a New Forest preserve, because there wasn't the slightest sign of habitation on either side. All Tracey could do was keep him talking until they reached a village or residential area.

Suddenly aware that Nigel was still waiting for an answer, she said, "Bart didn't tell me his business—if that's what you mean."

"It wasn't exactly what I had in mind," he drawled, "but I'll play it your way for now."

"Wasn't Herbie at Kensington High Street the next day, too?" she asked, hoping to get his mind out of the bedroom. It didn't occur to her until too late that it might have been safer to keep quiet about her near-accident with the bus.

"Could be." Nigel's eyes narrowed. "He helped me out from time to time. We were both a bit upset that day when you set the guv'nor on us. We'd been ticking along nicely with our business and didn't plan on having to change our schedule. Oh, I know you didn't intend to cause a fuss, love," he assured Tracey before she could protest. "That's why I'm being so nice to you now. Rather than losing my temper again." His clasp on her hand tightened and he smiled in satisfaction as she drew a breath of pain. "See what I mean?" He loosened his grip and spoke as if nothing had happened.

"No, I don't," she said, trying to stay in character. "I don't even like antiques, so why all this fuss about some miserable table?"

"Because we had a few too many of them stored about, that's why. I thought that you'd already asked your boyfriend about them. Wasn't that why you were searching the storeroom last night? Why you were at Ardsley in the first place?"

"You know that wasn't the real reason." She dropped her voice suggestively. "Everybody has to make a living. What's so strange about that? I thought that hiring out for banquet help was a nice touch."

"That wasn't what you told the housekeeper. The old lady was plenty surprised when I informed her you'd ended up in Jennings' bed."

Tracey closed her eyes, wishing she could close out the image of Mrs. Jenks' horrified expression, as well. Her voice was subdued when she finally managed to ask, "Where are you taking me?"

"Just for a bit of a ride. Mind you, we could make it a longer trip if you cooperate."

The undertone in his voice made Tracey decide to drop the role she'd been attempting. If she kept insisting that she was Bart's girlfriend, Nigel would certainly get ideas of his own. If his tone were anything to go by, he was already more than half-convinced.

"Right now, the only thing that appeals to me is a coffee house," she said in forthright fashion. "I didn't stop for breakfast before I left Ardsley."

"Sorry, love—"

"I wish you'd stop calling me that," she said, cutting into his words. "I'm not your love and I don't intend to be."

"Well, now"—his clasp tightened again warningly—"who flipped your switch? You shouldn't contradict a man when he's talking to you so nice and mannerly. Besides, you might be very happy to be going along with me. I've always heard it's better on top of the Channel rather than under it."

"What do you mean?"

Tracey's frightened whisper seemed to bring real enjoyment to the man beside her. "Interested, are you?" he asked. "I thought you might be. Well, since we're getting so close, I'll lay it out. All this snooping around made me decide to take the lolly and run. There's a friend of mine with a cruiser near Southampton, and he's giving us a trip across the Channel to stay with friends of mine on the Continent."

"Us? You mean . . . you and me?"

"And a few of the lads who've been helping me. You see, they didn't bother to consult Her Majesty's Immigration when they came over to work here, so they'll have to go back where they came from—for the moment. You'd better keep your mouth shut about it when we meet up with them. They're not apt to be as forgiving as I am. But then"—he took his hand away from hers long enough to smooth his mustache—"they're only interested in reproducing furniture. Now, the entire process of reproduction fascinates me."

Sheer unmitigated fury lashed through Tracey at his last words. She glared at him as he drove on, whistling softly through his teeth. It would be a cold day in hell, she vowed, before she let that cretin set a hand on her. If only she knew where he was eventually going to stop the car, she could try for a way to escape. In the meantime, she'd better keep her aversion hidden.

"I wish we could get something to eat," she said, thinking if she harped on the subject long enough, he might detour into a town. "It couldn't hurt to stop for a minute. Even Mr. Rustad wouldn't blame you for bending the rules a little more, would he?"

"Well, now, I didn't think to ask him before I left, and I doubt that we'll have much communication in the future. Your chum Jennings brought about that state of affairs." Nigel shot a quick sideways glance in her direction. Her puzzled face made him burst into laughter. "Lord love us—you didn't really imagine the mighty Oliver was doing a bunk, too?"

Tracey was so confused that for a moment she forgot about the trouble she was in. "You mean that Mr. Rustad isn't in this with you. Any part of it?"

"Hardly, love. That stiff-necked fool wouldn't break with tradition even if he starved. Imagine mucking about with tourist banquets and tours when he's living in a bloody treasure chest. He could have made a fortune if he'd listened to me."

"But he didn't," Tracey said, finally figuring it out. "I suppose when he spent so much time abroad, it made it even easier for you and your friends."

"It helped."

"He must really have been surprised when Bart told him about a choice Regency worktable for sale in the Kensington Arcade and mentioned your name."

"It was a bit dicey, but I managed to stall him with an excuse about a wrong delivery." Nigel seemed amused by her attempt at deduction. "I like a woman who takes an interest in higher finance. As long as she has other assets—like yours. Now, my dear, I can't promise you any coffee, but there's a good chance for a nice cup of tea when we get round that bend of the road," he said, sounding like an expansive host.

"You mean there's a restaurant ahead?" Tracey sat up straighter in her seat and peered eagerly through the windshield. "I wouldn't have thought there'd be one out here in the middle of the forest."

He braked slightly around the curve. "Right you are—but there might be a tea flask in the cab of that lorry parked beside the footpath."

"That's what you were talking about?" Her voice was sick with disappointment. "Just a parked truck?"

"Exactly. I keep forgetting you're an American," he said, pulling to a stop about twenty feet behind the high-curtained tailgate. "We loaded it last night with a few of Oliver's choicer originals. That way, we can keep our hand in when we get on the other side of the Channel. You'll be glad to know that your favorite worktable is there, too." He took the key out of the ignition and put it in his pants pocket. "I'll go up and have a word with my chaps—if we linger here too long, they might come back to investigate on their own, and I don't think you'd like that."

His tone was without emphasis but there was such an ominous light in his hooded eyes that Tracey shrank back in her seat, watching him get out of the car without saying a word.

He lingered for a moment longer. "Don't try anything foolish, love. I told them to post a lookout, so you wouldn't get far before somebody came after you. Mind you, I wouldn't like to say what would happen then." His empty smile flashed as if he'd just conferred her with honors. "Be good and I'll bring you a nice cuppa. Sweets to the sweet, I always say."

That banality was left for an exit line as he slammed his car door and strode up the side of the road toward the parked truck.

Tracey didn't waste a moment twisting in her seat to see if there was anything in the back of the car that she could use to defend herself when he returned. Her glance lit on some tools which had been thrown carelessly on the floor behind the driver's seat, and she bent down to frantically rummage through them. She gave a pleased exclamation when she discovered a sharp wood chisel, and picked it up gingerly, avoiding its razor-sharp metal edges. Carefully keeping it below dashboard level, she transferred it to the front seat, and then she looked up to gauge Nigel's progress. He was almost up to the cab of the truck, glancing back over his shoulder to check on her at that very moment.

Her immobile figure must have pleased him, because he nodded with satisfaction and turned to go on his way.

Tracey didn't wait any longer. She reached for her door handle the instant he turned away and was out of the car, clutching the chisel at her side and running like a woman possessed toward the waist-high undergrowth across the road.

She'd only gone a few feet before she heard a shout of alarm and then a shot rang out from the front of the truck. Tracey lunged through the bushes, trying desperately to get out of sight before the man reached her.

Ten seconds later, pounding footsteps and crashing brush told her that she hadn't succeeded—someone was on her heels and gaining. She let out an anguished sob and turned like a cornered animal, bringing up the sharp wood chisel as a last frantic measure. An instant later she felt it being yanked from her nerveless fingers as she stumbled, half-fainting, into Bart Jennings' arms.

She wasn't conscious of anything for a minute or so afterward except that he held her in a powerful embrace which showed no signs of weakening, even when she took a deep, shuddering breath and lifted her head.

"Tracey, you damned little fool," he was saying over and over again in a rough voice, proving that he wasn't in much better shape than she was.

"Don't remind me," she whispered, trying to wipe tears from her cheeks with the back of her hand until he pushed it away and did the job with his handkerchief. When he'd finished, she said, "I've never been so terrified in my life. I was sure it was Nigel behind me . . ." Her eyes dilated suddenly as she remembered. "That gang at the truck . . . Oh, God, they'll come after us!"

"Stop it!" Bart commanded, giving her a sharp shake. "You don't have to worry anymore. They're already under arrest."

"And Nigel?"

"He's right with them."

"But that shot I heard . . ."

". . . Came when he tried to get away. The police had been waiting for him to appear at the truck so they could wrap up the case. We'd been sitting there most of the night for just that. But I don't give a damn about him," Bart said unevenly. "I've been going out of my mind ever since the constables at Ardsley radioed that Nigel had picked you up on the road. How could you manage such a foolish stunt?" he began, and then broke off at the misery in her face. "I'm sorry," he said pulling her close against him again. "I didn't mean to rake you over the coals. It's just that I've been so damned scared."

"Oh, I know," she said, burrowing into his shirt-front. "I feel the same way. I couldn't believe it when it turned out to be you—to think I might have hurt you . . ." she added incoherently. "That awful chisel!"

He took her hand and dropped a soft kiss on her fingertips. "Darling idiot! You're not the Lizzie Borden type, so stop worrying."

She managed to smile in response, even though she stayed close in his protective clasp.

Bart had been watching her anxiously, and her smile made his own spirits soar in relief. Enough to make him add lightly, "It's a good thing I vouched for you earlier. Otherwise, the local constabulary would have some questions to ask about your keeping company with friend Nigel."

She stared up at him, shocked. "They can't think that I wanted to be with him."

"Not now. I told them that you were probably hitching a ride back to Southampton when he picked you up."

"But how did you know?"

He gave her a quick, impulsive squeeze. "Because I'm finally beginning to realize how that ridiculous mind of yours works. Fortunately, Nigel followed his prescribed trail, too. The police were sure that he'd appear here for the rendezvous with his men and bring you along."

"Thank heaven he did. I must have been the only person around who *didn't* know what was going on. Of course. I didn't get much help."

"That's what happens to independent women." He flicked the end of her nose with a derisive finger. "Don't try hitting me—you haven't the strength for it yet."

"I hadn't any intention of hitting you," she said, not quite truthfully. "Besides, I know all about Nigel's scheme now. He told me in the car."

"Did he mention how he'd set up a nice little ring to copy Oliver's choicer pieces of furniture and later sell them abroad for equally choice prices?"

"He rambled on about parts of it," she said, enjoying her triumph, "when he could keep his mind on business."

"God! He didn't hurt you, did he?"

"Oh, no! It was all talk," Tracey hastened to reassure Bart. "He was offering me a trip across the Channel and telling me what a great time we'd have together. After last night, he seemed to be impressed by my experience along that line."

"And you let him believe it? You were a damned little fool! It's lucky he kept his mind on business long enough to get here." Bart gave her a concerned glance. "We'd better go back to the car. There'll be plenty of time to talk about it later. Can you walk to the road, or shall I carry you?"

"I can walk, thanks." She wasn't sure that she was hearing right and she didn't dare ask Bart to repeat what he'd called her. "Darling idiot" and "damned little fool" weren't found in love sonnets, but on the other hand, Bart Jennings wasn't the sonnet type. Just then, he looked exhausted, and he'd obviously spent the night in his clothes, but she realized suddenly she wouldn't trade the grave concern of his glances for a million dollars.

She felt a sudden warmth speed through her, as if her emotions were thawing after a long winter. Turning her head, she noted that the stark surroundings of the Forest, which had looked so forbidding earlier, actually were alive with beauty. Up above sparrows were winging between two sturdy oak trees, their small shapes making dark streaks against the pale morning sky until they reached the sheltering branches. Even the desolate mist that had shrouded the countryside in early morning had been burned off by sunshine, and a homely earthen smell rose from underfoot. Tracey took a deep, steadying breath, glad that she'd surfaced to reality again.

Bart kept a grip on her hand as he moved ahead of her, saying, "Better let me go first, or this undergrowth will tear your clothes."

"Then lay on, MacDuff."

He grinned companionably over his shoulder. "Your history's off again—you're in the wrong part of the country for that quote."

She was stumbling along behind him on the rough ground. "I know—and you're not MacDuff, so I've got the wrong man, too. But all things considered . . ."

He hesitated, strangely intent as he looked back at her. "All things considered?"

"I'll keep the one I have," she said demurely.

After that it wasn't long until the waist-high growth changed to grass stubble, and Bart pulled her up alongside him as they reached the road. The truck had already been moved off, and the only remnants of officialdom were two policemen who were just getting in Nigel's parked car.

"It looks as if we almost have the place to ourselves," Bart said. "Do you want to wait while I check with them and get my car? It's parked in the trees up there around the bend."

"Will I have to give a statement or anything?" Tracey asked, thankful that all the other reminders of the morning were out of sight.

"I shouldn't think so, but we can go and see," Bart said calmly as he led her over to talk to the officers.

The two constables couldn't have been nicer, and assured Tracey that they would be in touch with her later to get a deposition. They waited until Bart had retrieved his car and then helped Tracey into it, waving them off like old friends.

It was the same sports car that Tracey had seen at Winchester. She couldn't help asking, "Doesn't Stella mind? When you use this car, I mean?"

"I don't see why she should, since I rented it." He grinned at her. "Are you putting two and two together to make five again?"

"I hope so." She bit her lip. "I saw you both at the cathedral in Winchester yesterday afternoon."

"Why didn't you come over or set off a rocket or something? Oh, I get it—you were wondering about that enthusiastic greeting of Stella's." Bart accelerated to pass a cyclist and then moved back to his side of the road. "Well, you can't blame her for being excited. She'd just settled on a wedding date." A dead silence followed his remark, and Bart turned to bestow a puzzled look on Tracey. As her pale, stricken face registered, he abruptly drew over to the side of the road and stopped. "Stella's going to marry Oliver, you little idiot! She had to confirm their wedding date at the cathedral, and I was the only one who was free to drive her over yesterday afternoon. It wasn't much out of my way. I'd been trying to get in touch with you at that bed-and-breakfast place."

Tracey felt relief flow through her at his words. "How did you know where to look for me?"

"You aren't the only person who knows how to tip a taxi driver, my girl." He grinned at her. "What do you say we find a more comfortable place for explanations. There's a nice little picnic spot down the road here a mile or so. Okay?"

"It sounds heavenly," she agreed, and watched him accelerate out on the road again. "If you could conjure up a picnic lunch to go with the place, I'd be your slave for life."

"I'll make a note of that. In the meantime, you can reach behind the seat for that basket on the floor."

"Do you mean it?" She brought a reed basket up to her lap and opened the top excitedly, pulling out a flask and a foil-wrapped pouch. "Hot coffee and buttered rolls! Bart, you're an absolute genius!"

"Well, it's taken you long enough to discover it. Why in hell didn't I think of furnishing a picnic lunch earlier? Imagine what I could have accomplished with you by now!"

"You haven't done badly. We're going to have to share this cup."

"I plan on sharing more than that. Here we are— will you join me for breakfast, madam?" He pulled off the road with a flourish and stopped in a sunny open spot by a grove of oak trees. Nearby, a stream meandered lazily, edging a parklike meadow. Bart got out and came around to help Tracey, taking the basket in his other hand. "Would you prefer two flat rocks where we can be alone, or that stump nearer the orchestra?"

"The dance floor looks a little crowded, so I'll take the rocks, please."

"Better and better," he said, leading her over to the sunny rocks near the bank of the stream and putting the picnic basket within easy reach. "Think of the money we'll save on our entertainment budget. For that, you can have first chance at the coffee." He stretched out at her side and helped himself to a roll after tossing another one in her lap. "You'll notice that I'm being the perfect gentleman."

"I *had* noticed," she commented, trying to look judicial as she ate. "Of course, I could mention that it was about time."

Bart turned up his shirt collar and pretended to shiver. "The breeze is turning chilly. It was a mistake giving you that food—you were easier to control as a weak little woman."

She smiled but she had trouble keeping her lips steady as she poured more coffee in the cup and handed it to him. "It's hard to joke about it even now. Do you know, this is the first time I can remember when everything's perfect. It's like coming back to life again after dying a little on that ride with Nigel. The night before wasn't too good, either," she added, fixing Bart with a stern eye. "Leaving me locked in your bedroom without my clothes was a miserable trick."

"That was done with malice aforethought." He handed the cup back to her and rested on his elbow again. "Also with the best of intentions. I wanted you safely out of the way while we tried to get Nigel and his chums together with all of the Ardsley furnishings they'd stolen. Oliver and I had been working with the police ever since you'd mentioned the worktable in London. He and Stella had just become engaged, so naturally she came down here, too."

"Naturally. You might have mentioned that fact before this," Tracey pointed out.

"When? You did a disappearing act in London, and that made me mad." His slow grin taunted her. "Whenever I mentioned Stella, you gave off sparks like the Fourth of July."

"That's because I wanted to scratch her eyes out. I thought you kissed me in that hotel to make her jealous."

Bart shook his head. "No way. I was looking for an excuse to kiss you, and there it was."

"And last night? The interlude on the bed?" Tracey plucked a piece of grass and kept her attention on it as she twirled it between her thumb and finger. "Was that because of Nigel?"

Bart waited until her eyes finally came up to meet his, and then he chose his words carefully. "It started that way, but two seconds after he'd closed the door, I'd forgotten all about him. Leaving you on that bed was the hardest thing I've ever had to do in my life."

Tracey's heart pounded as their glances held. Bart's words told her that he was remembering every moment of their lovemaking, and his disturbing look was promising it wouldn't be long until it was repeated.

His next words confirmed it. "Incidentally, I don't intend to leave when I get you on my bed the next time, so we'd better get married damned fast."

She drew an ecstatic breath and then found that

she had to reach for his handkerchief again to wipe her eyes.

"That's enough of that," Bart told her, mopping her cheeks gently. "Fine thing! The first time I've proposed marriage to a woman, and she starts to cry. What's that supposed to mean?"

"It means that I'd love to marry you," she assured him in a wobbly voice.

"It's a good thing. I could see the handwriting on the wall the first morning you spilled the coffee." He sighed with mock dismay and stuffed the handkerchief back in his pocket. "Imagine waiting all this time to fall in love with a redhead."

"One with sexual fantasies," she reminded him. "I've been afraid to go to sleep ever since."

"Well, I had to say something to keep you around. I couldn't keep feeding you all the time, and there wasn't anything better to do then."

"But there is now?" Tracey kept her hands folded demurely in her lap.

Bart's grin wiped all the tiredness from his face. "You're damned right! Nigel's finally in the local jail, and Oliver has all his furniture back—plus a few extra pieces. Stella has her man, and now she can run medieval banquets to her heart's content. You, my dearest one, will tell Oscar that you're resigning to do research for a much more hardhearted employer."

"And if Oscar objects?" Tracey asked, her voice provocative.

"Then we'll send him a splendid Regency worktable as a consolation present, because Oliver now has quite a collection of them. I think that takes care of all the unimportant things," Bart concluded. He reached across and pulled her down against him. "Now . . . come here, woman."

There was only an instant for Tracey to recognize the dangerous timbre in his voice before he'd pulled her close, molding her against his long length as he bent to kiss her.

After that, there was no time to think. The world became an enchanted place as passion surfaced in both of them, igniting physical responses and needs that were hard to control and even harder to check.

When they finally drew apart, Bart spoke with an urgency that Tracey hadn't heard before. "That's why I didn't dare keep you in my arms last night," he told her. "I can't even think straight when I'm near you. All I can say is that I love every bit of you—I want you like hell—and we'd better find out about getting married right away." The last was said as he got determinedly to his feet, pulling her up in the same motion.

Tracey was almost as breathless as he was, but she managed to keep her tone solemn. "It just happens that I remember the way to Winchester Cathedral."

"So do I." Bart's grin flashed again as he urged her toward the car. "Let's go give them our business."

About the Author

Glenna Finley is a native of Washington State. She earned her degree from Stanford University in Russian Studies and in Speech and Dramatic Arts, with emphasis on radio.

After a stint in radio and publicity work in Seattle, she went to New York City to work for NBC as a producer in its international division. In addition, she worked with the "March of Time" and *Life* magazine.

As a producer, she had her own show about activities in Manhattan, a show that was broadcast to England. The programs were similar to those of the "Voice of America."

Though her life in New York was exciting, she eventually returned to the Northwest where she married. Currently residing in Seattle with her husband, Donald Witte, and their son, she loves to travel, and draws heavily on her travels and experiences for the novels that have been published. Her books for NAL have sold several million copies.

𝒮

SIGNET Books You'll Enjoy

Buy them at your local

bookstore or use coupon

on next page for ordering.

More Romance from SIGNET

- [ ] **SIGNET DOUBLE ROMANCE—WEB OF ENCHANTMENT** by Claudia Slack and **OUTRAGEOUS FORTUNE** by Claudia Slack. (#J9357—$1.95)
- [ ] **SIGNET DOUBLE ROMANCE: DANGER IN MONTPARNASSE** by Hermina Black and **THE LORDSHIP OF LOVE** by Hermina Black. (#E8832—$1.75)*
- [ ] **SIGNET DOUBLE ROMANCE: THE RED LADY** by Katharine Newlin Burt and **HIDDEN CREEK** by Katharine Newlin Burt. (#J8861—$1.95)*
- [ ] **SHADOW OF LOVE** by Kristin Michaels. (#W8901—$1.50)*
- [ ] **THE MAGIC SIDE OF THE MOON** by Kristin Michaels. (#W8712—$1.50)*
- [ ] **ENCHANTED TWILIGHT** by Kristin Michaels. (#Y7733—$1.25)
- [ ] **A SPECIAL KIND OF LOVE** by Kristin Michaels. (#Y7039—$1.25)
- [ ] **TO BEGIN WITH LOVE** by Kristin Michaels. (#Y7732—$1.25)
- [ ] **HEARTSONG** by Kristin Michaels. (#E9212—$1.75)
- [ ] **LOVE AT SEA** by Maxine Patrick. (#E9261—$1.75)*
- [ ] **CAPTIVE KISSES** by Maxine Patrick. (#E9425—$1.75)
- [ ] **SNOWBOUND HEART** by Maxine Patrick. (#E8935—$1.75)
- [ ] **BAYOU BRIDE** by Maxine Patrick. (#E8527—$1.75)*

*Price slightly higher in Canada

𝒪
_____

SIGNET Double Romances for the Price of One!

☐ **SIGNET DOUBLE ROMANCE—FOLLOW THE HEART** by Heather Sinclair and **FOR THE LOVE OF A STRANGER** by Heather Sinclair. (#J8363—$1.95)*

☐ **SIGNET DOUBLE ROMANCE—IT HAPPENED IN SPAIN** by Ivy Valdes and **CRISTINA'S FANTASY** by Ivy Valdes. (#E7983—$1.75)

☐ **SIGNET DOUBLE ROMANCE—GIFT FROM A STRANGER** by Ivy Valdes and **OVER MY SHOULDER** by Ivy Valdes. (#E8181—$1.75)

☐ **SIGNET DOUBLE ROMANCE—SHEILA'S DILEMMA** by Ivy Valdes and **THE INTRUSION** by Elizabeth McCrae. (#W7440—$1.50)†

☐ **SIGNET DOUBLE ROMANCE—THE DAWN OF LOVE** by Teri Lester and **TANIA** by Teri Lester. (#E7804—$1.75)

☐ **SIGNET DOUBLE ROMANCE—A CONFLICT OF WOMEN** by Emma Darby and **HAVEN OF PEACE** by I. Torr. (#W7370—$1.50)

☐ **SIGNET DOUBLE ROMANCE—LOVING YOU ALWAYS** by Peggy Gaddis and **THE GIRL NEXT DOOR** by Peggy Gaddis. (#Y6760—$1.25)

☐ **SIGNET DOUBLE ROMANCE—RETURN TO LOVE** by Peggy Gaddis and **ENCHANTED SPRING** by Peggy Gaddis. (#W7158—$1.50)

☐ **SIGNET DOUBLE ROMANCE—SECRET HONEYMOON** by Peggy Gaddis and **HANDFUL OF MIRACLES** by Marion Naismith. (#Y6761—$1.25)

*Price slightly higher in Canada
† Not available in Canada

_____

Buy them at your local

bookstore or use coupon

on next page for ordering.